THE REDEEMED

by

Jonas Saul

PUBLISHED BY:
Imagine Press Inc.
Ebook ISBN: 978-1-927404-36-2
Paperback ISBN: 978-1-998047-33-8
Hardcover ISBN: 978-1-998047-34-5

The Redeemed
Copyright © 2014 by Jonas Saul

The Decoy (Thirty-Three)
The Disappearance (Thirty-Four)
The Whole Truth (Thirty-Five)
Alex (Thirty-Six)
Parkman (Thirty-Seven)
Darwin (Thirty-Eight)
Aaron (Thirty-Nine)
Remains To Be Seen (Forty)

The Jake Wood Novels

The Immortal Gene (Book One)
The Immortal Target (Book Two)

Standalone Novels

'Til Death Do Us Part
The Drowning
The Woman in the Woods
The Threat
The Specter
The Mafia Trilogy
A Murder in Time
Frequency of the Dead

Co-Authored Novels

Collision Course (Written with Gary Ponzo)
There Will Be Blood (Written with Rania Stone)
The Soulless (Written with Rania Stone)

Short Story Collections

Twisted Fate (Tales of Horror)

Twists of Fate (Tales of Hope)

Chapter 1

Sarah Roberts leaned on her crutch as she stood over the decapitated and mutilated body of what was once a man. Written on the note in her hand were her sister's words. The message was specific, but it meant nothing to Sarah.

Gaspard de Coligny. Everybody and everything has its time.

"What is it?" Parkman asked.

"Nothing, really."

Sarah covered her nose as a breeze came up and ushered the thick stench of the dead priest toward her. Crime scene investigators combed the wooded and grassy area of Mulholland Drive where the body had been found. The scattered lights of Los Angeles below covered the landscape as if a giant had spread them out like diamonds on a velvet cloth. The call to her hotel room came over an hour ago. Another body. Another murder.

Before Detective David Hirst would allow the body to be taken away, he wanted the head found. Detective Hirst also delayed because he wanted Father Adams to examine the victim. There was a chance Adams would be able to ID the body. The previous four men murdered in the city in the last eight days had been Catholic priests, all known to Father Adams.

Since Parkman and Sarah arrived from Canada yesterday, Detective David Hirst had brought them up to speed on the case. Four dead bodies so far, and he anticipated more. All Catholic priests from different areas of Los Angeles, The City of Angels. All four dead bodies bore a cross with the victim's name engraved along the wooden spine. Each body had the cross nailed into the chest plate.

"Anything?" Detective Hirst moved closer to Sarah and Parkman. "Can your sister help?"

Sarah shook her head and caught the glimpse Hirst shot Parkman.

She crumpled the note in her hand, eased it into her pocket, then pivoted on the crutch and hobbled toward the darkness between two street lights. Footsteps bounded behind her.

"Sarah?" Parkman said.

She kept walking. She needed to be away from this place. The men had work to do, evidence to gather. Unless she could help, there was no point standing around the crime scene.

"Sarah, everyone's under a lot of pressure," Parkman said from a few steps behind.

She wheeled around to face him. The streetlight cast a warm glow across his features, and she saw his age for the first time in a while. The bags under his eyes revealed his lack of sleep. The nervous tick he had developed lately said volumes about his stress level. The toothpick in his mouth was aged and fraying, yet he clutched it like an old friend.

Sarah hadn't received a single note from Vivian except the one crumpled up in her pocket. She knew Hirst was wondering how much help the psychic girl would be. It had only been an hour since the note in her pocket was written. Maybe it wasn't only Sarah who didn't enjoy working with the police. Maybe Vivian held a certain dislike for authorities as well.

"This isn't working," Sarah said, a slight ache rising in her shattered ankle. They had repaired it to the point where she could walk again in eight to ten weeks, but that didn't help right now. Calluses had formed in the palms of her hands after working with the crutches. Tonight she only had one crutch.

"We had to try." Parkman glanced over his shoulder, then back to Sarah. "*I* had to try. I owe David. I felt we could help. He's really stuck. He has nothing to go on."

"Parkman, I've seen a lot of dead bodies in my time, even caused a few, but I've never seen what was done to that man. His head was cut off. His hands and feet were hacked off, and his genitals were missing. Your detective friend isn't looking for a crazy serial killer. He's looking for an angry one. The killer is filled with rage. He's evil incarnate. Lucifer has a special place for this person in Hell if there is a Hell."

Parkman stepped closer. "That's why we have to help."

Sarah adjusted herself on the crutch. "It's funny."

"What's funny?"

"I would love to help, but without Vivian, I'm stuck,

too."

"I know that."

"But they don't." She nodded toward the men gathered around the crime scene. "I want to help. This murderer is a crazed lunatic. But there's nothing I can do until Vivian gives me something to go on. People forget I'm not psychic. It's Vivian who works the magic. I spend most of my time trying to stay alive."

Parkman moved in and wrapped his arms around her. "I know," he whispered. "If Vivian gives you nothing, we'll leave. If your hands are tied, then they are tied. There's no way around that." He leaned back but kept his hands on her shoulders, his head bowed. "At least we came down to L.A. and gave it a shot."

"What was that look between you and Hirst?"

He released her shoulders and stepped back. "You know how the boys in blue look at you. Some of them resent that a woman in her mid-twenties can access crime scenes without proper schooling or training. The rest of them don't believe in psychic abilities. You're in a no-win situation with most of these guys—"

"C'mon, Parkman. That's not it at all. Most of these guys hate me because of my anti-cop reputation. Considering what just went down in Canada, I can see why."

"That was cleared up. The media ran the stories of how Barry Ashford was murdered and the crimes he and his wife were responsible for. It wasn't enough that he was a cop. He lost all credibility when the truth came out."

Sarah cleared her throat. "Some of these guys," she gestured at the dozen men in suits and uniforms, "haven't read everything in the paper. All they know is that I went to

Canada to hunt a cop down, and after I kidnapped him, he was tortured and murdered."

"These guys aren't stupid, Sarah. They know that if you were responsible for that in any way, you wouldn't be here right now helping with this investigation. You'd be behind bars."

"I don't know why it's bothering me so much. Normally I wouldn't care. But I came here to fix things and redeem myself with the authorities and you."

The building to her right caught her eye. Perimeter lights glowed along its white walls, and a large parking lot spread out on the other side of the building.

"What's that place?" Sarah asked to change the subject, overly frustrated by Vivian, how the case was being handled and having to deal with crutches.

"I overheard one of the officers say it's a Protestant or Presbyterian church. Something like that."

"Isn't it interesting that the killer engraves the names of his victims?" She met Parkman's gaze. "Catholic priests, on a cross and leaves his most recent kill fifty yards from a church?"

Parkman shrugged. "Sarah, we're not here to deduce facts, to examine the evidence, or to be concerned about the killer's motivation. We're here to give Detective Hirst something only you can offer him. If you can't, that's okay too." He glanced down at the pocket that held the crumpled note. "What was that paper in your hand earlier when you were by the body?"

"A note from Vivian. She caught me in the hotel before coming out here."

"Sounds promising." He raised his eyebrows. "What did

she say?"

"That everything would come in its time."

"Okay, maybe that means she'll give you something Hirst can work with soon. In its time."

"Maybe. But I'm worried about something."

"What's that?"

"The first four victims were Catholic priests with a reputation for doing things they weren't supposed to be doing."

"We don't know that. Sure, two of them were transferred from Boston after allegations they had abused children, but nothing has been proven in court."

"I'm not worried about what can be proven in court or not. If they touched children inappropriately in any way, they deserve to be castrated and then killed. Especially men in such a position of trust. And we're not talking about a father figure or an employer. We're talking about a man of God here. That is a horrid crime."

She adjusted her collar as the air seemed to thicken around her. The opinion she had of organized religion was one of acceptance. Her opinion of predators who prey on weak and helpless children from a position of trust was one of extreme prejudice. Whoever preyed on the children of the human race didn't deserve to be a part of that race anymore.

"So what are you saying, Sarah? You don't want to stop these murders if the men being killed, whether priests or not, are criminals?"

"I'm a vigilante. I go after people and stop them, or at least try to before they hurt others. That's why I'm here. But what if I'm tasked to stop a vigilante? How would Vivian respond? In essence, aren't I attempting to stop the exact thing that I have become? Maybe that was why Vivian said that everybody and everything has its time. Maybe this is the priests' time to pay for their wrongdoings."

"Let me get this straight. Are you condoning murder?"

"Come on, Parkman. You know what I'm saying."

"Just bouncing it back and forth. I need to know if we're done in this city. If that's Vivian's position, then maybe we are."

Sarah watched the men gathered around the body. "No, we're not done yet. The last message from her was too recent."

A four-door sedan came up the road and parked six cars down from their car. The engine died. The vehicle caught the attention of several officers. After a moment, the driver's side door opened. A man got out wearing a long black coat. He reached back inside the car and withdrew, a hat in his hand.

"Is this the Father Adams I've been hearing about?" Sarah asked.

"Probably."

"Poor guy. He's been busy identifying the bodies of his priests. Wonder what kind of sermon one could write about that."

The man started across the grass, headed for the crime scene, each step seemingly calculated and assessed. He was a tall man. Sarah pegged him as slightly over six feet. His coat went to mid-calf, and his hat's brim kept his face shrouded in shadow. If he weren't a man of the cloth, he would come across as someone very rich, someone used to the taste of money. There was an air about him, one of regal confidence, as if Prince Charles were walking toward the officers simply to ask directions to the local pub.

"Where do they get guys like this?" Sarah asked.

"No idea."

"Since someone is targeting priests, maybe we should learn a little more about the Catholic church."

"You can't become a specialist in everything. There just isn't enough time. That's why they bring specialists in."

"That's not what I meant," Sarah said. "I meant, let's go back to the dead body and listen to what Father Adams has to say."

"Oh," Parkman said, but Sarah was already hobbling past him, moving fast on her one crutch.

Two officers crowded around Father Adams as he stood over the body. Sarah limped to the side and stood near the victim's legs. Detective Hirst afforded her a small nod, then stared at Father Adams. Everyone waited. Sarah felt Parkman's presence behind her.

"And you are?" Father Adams spoke without looking up, his voice deep, resonant.

Probably from years of sermons.

Since no one answered right away, Sarah assumed he was addressing her. "I'm nobody," Sarah said. "Don't worry yourself about me. I'm sure you have more important things on your plate. Or, at your feet, to be sure."

Father Adams hesitated a moment longer, then slowly looked up. The hat kept most of the top half of his face in shadow, but Sarah could see his left eye. If the human eye could detect education, money, and stature, this man possessed that ocular device. There was intelligence in his face, a greater intelligence that belied his position with the church. One would expect this kind of man to be a cardinal in the Sistine Chapel, voting for the next pope or maybe the pope himself. Not a priest in Los Angeles attempting to save the souls of a few.

"How do you find yourself here?" he asked. "What is your purpose?"

"Same as yours."

"And that is?"

"You're not sure why you're here?" Sarah asked.

She detected Parkman adjust himself from one foot to the other behind her. No one else moved. Detective Hirst and his men were quiet in the Father's presence as if a man of God held divine powers over humans. Sarah held the utmost respect for belief systems and faith and was quite a spiritual person herself, but organized religion had never enticed her.

Father Adams's head lowered. He studied the body at his feet. A moment later, he crouched down and took a closer look.

"This appears to be the body of Father Alvin. He wasn't seen at his church today. I worried you would locate another body soon." Adams got to his feet. "Locating the head would allow for certainty, but this is most surely Father Alvin. I saw him two days ago. He wore these same pants."

"How can you be so certain?" Sarah asked.

Detective Hirst shot her a cautious glance. All it did was make her want to ask more questions. Wasn't that what she was here for? Don't ask Parkman to bring her along as a favor, then try to quell her when she shows up.

"Father Alvin doesn't shirk his responsibilities. His commitment to the church is quite sound. Missing from his church all day isn't a habit of his."

Sarah turned and hobbled away on the one crutch. Behind her, she heard Father Adams ask, "Detective Hirst, who was that girl?"

"Her name is Sarah Roberts. I asked her to join us."

"And why is that?" Adams asked.

"She has a certain insight into these kinds of things."

Then she was too far away to discern anything more other than the sound of their voices.

"What was that all about?" Parkman asked as he caught up to her. "It almost sounded like you were challenging the guy."

"I don't trust him," Sarah said as she slowed down to catch her breath. Walking with a crutch was hard on the uneven ground.

"Who do you trust?" Parkman asked, his voice lined with sarcasm.

"Exactly."

They returned to their rental car, where Sarah inserted her crutch through the open back window and dropped into the passenger seat. Parkman walked around and got in behind the wheel.

"Why does trust have to come into it when dealing with a priest?" Parkman asked. "As a man of God, aren't we all supposed to respect them, trust them?"

"You're right. What is there to trust about a priest? All I know about their religion is what I've seen on TV, like the horrific molestations. It isn't fair to judge them all based on that, though."

Parkman started the car. "Coffee?"

She shook her head and stared out the window at the men gathered in the dark. Father Adams had broken away from the group and was returning to his car. "No, it'll keep me awake. I want wine and then my bed. Research tomorrow.

We've got two days until another priest is murdered based on the going rate. Unless Vivian gives me something soon, Hirst will ask us to leave in a couple of days since we're not helping."

Parkman pulled away from the curb as other vehicles showed up. "I'd agree with you on that."

"But there's something else."

"What's that?" Parkman asked.

"Why didn't Hirst tell Father Adams that the cross in this victim's chest had the name Alvin scratched into it?"

"Father Adams is the liaison to the church. Coming out tonight was a formality. They always need someone to identify the body."

"Fair enough, but something isn't adding up."

"What isn't adding up?"

"No idea, but I intend to find out."

Chapter 2

MIKE SAT IN HIS car, the engine idling. It was an old car with an operational cigarette lighter and a cassette deck. He popped the lighter, lit his cigarette, puffed hard, pulled the smoke deep into his lungs, and exhaled.

He grabbed the camera from the passenger seat, made sure the settings were right for the night shot without a flash and snapped a couple of pics of the retreating car with the woman on the crutch and her male companion. He would locate her again and get a proper picture of her face. Something for his collection.

In his opinion, you were either in the holy camp or the unholy camp. No one could be a part of both. Good people died and went to Heaven. Unholy people died and went to Hell. Just as the Rapture would snatch good people up in the glory of Heaven, so would he snatch unholy, evil people to the depths of Hell. One day he would sit next to Satan.

Mike was the chosen one, and only he knew it.

It was a fine line, though. He took pleasure in killing priests who had hurt children. The pleasure was a gift as everything unholy grew contrary to pleasure. Only the true God of Hell could take pleasure in the burning of souls.

Mike turned the car on when officers noticed him parked on the side of the road. Two men in uniforms walked toward him.

When Mike talked to Lucifer, he was promised a seat to the right of the Lord of the Flames if he could deliver the souls of God's representatives. That was what he intended to do for as long as he could. And anyone who attempted to stop him would die. The stupid girl and her friend just went on his picture board. A dozen years from now, the murders of Catholic priests would be nothing but a memory for the city of angels. But the murder of a girl on one crutch would be forgotten within a month.

He pulled away from the curb, performed a U-turn, passed the Presbyterian church, and headed downhill. The officers stopped walking, hesitated a moment, and turned back. They would probably assume he was a reporter who chickened out on getting the money shot because he didn't have a media badge or had decided that seeing the dead body would haunt his dreams.

Didn't matter. He got the shot he needed.

Next time he would snap a photo of that priest, Father Adams.

He couldn't imagine Adams was his real name. Who could be that high up in the Catholic church and share the name of that man from the Garden of Eden? What are the odds?

He smiled to himself in the rearview mirror. It was no different than the name of his girlfriend.

Evelyn Wynn.

He called her Eve.

As her personal apple, he tempted her all the time.

She was only eighteen, but the young ones were more gullible and more easily trained. And like a carrot to a horse or a bloody steak to a starving Doberman, women that young were drawn to cash, and he had enough to lure her away from the streets, away from her world.

He couldn't go to Hell without taking Eve with him.

In the rearview mirror, he saw his smiling reflection, the devilish curve of his mouth, and the homicidal fire in his eyes. Murder a priest, then fuck his girlfriend, the prostitute. Murder a priest, then be gifted for it.

Maybe when he murdered the girl on the crutch, he could do her, too.

His smile widened as he puffed on the remains of his cigarette.

The road to Hell was paved with good intentions, and he had enough good intentions to fill a football stadium. Preferably with whores. All are under the age of eighteen, just waiting to be deflowered.

But first, he had to kill another priest.

The asbestos chamber was ready.

He wondered how it would feel for the next priest as he was gassed and burned alive just like the Catholic Ustashi did in Croatia during World War II. Anton Pavelic, also known as the Butcher of the Balkans, was a practicing Catholic and a regular visitor of the pope during the 1940s. He ran a brutal extermination camp that burned its victims alive, killing over half a million people during the war. Many of the murderers were Franciscan Friars in what came to be known as the Vatican Holocaust.

The Roman Catholic church is the oldest corporation on Earth. They're also the most evil with their lies, murder, genocide, slavery, and hatred, not to mention how they handle pedophiles internally. Who better to send directly to Hell than the men representing this organization? It would have been shut down centuries ago if it were any other company. But not the Catholic church.

No, because the church has always worked for Lucifer. It's his wickedest deception, his great and secret performance.

A little research and Mike had all he needed to murder Catholic priests.

A little more research and he would know who the girl with the crutch was.

Everything Lucifer promised would be his.

He took a right on Beverly Glen Boulevard and headed to the parking lot where Eve worked. Tonight she would be his, and he would make sure she didn't work the streets ever again. It was time to have the whore all to himself.

He loved the sight of himself and smirked in the mirror once more.

How could being so evil feel so good?

Lucifer was right. Everything bad just tasted better.

Even Eve.

Chapter 3

THE LOS ANGELES SUN beat down hard, pressed past the curtains, violating Sarah's hotel room. Even with the curtains pulled tight and the air conditioner on full, the heat pressed on her as she lay in bed. Sleep had been elusive after last night's interruption.

Parkman hadn't knocked on the adjoining room's door yet. He was either still sleeping or gone for breakfast.

She got up, leaned heavily on her crutch, and headed to the kitchenette. She started the in-room coffeemaker and then fired up her MacBook Pro at the desk. After logging onto the hotel's WiFi, she pulled Vivian's note from her pants pocket and typed the man's name into Google.

Gaspard de Coligny, a Protestant leader, was assassinated on August 24, 1572, in the most brutal fashion. She read how he was killed and then understood why Vivian had given her this note.

It was a guide, a flashlight in the dark. Vivian was pointing the way. The only problem was her timing. It was too late.

Someone knocked on the door.

"I'll be a minute," she shouted.

Sarah moved to the bed and gingerly slipped into the track pants she used when lounging in the hotel room. Then she hobbled over and poured the coffee at the little kitchenette.

The knock came again.

She sipped her coffee and then stepped closer to the door. "Who is it?"

"Detective David Hirst."

"Parkman's in the other room."

"I came to talk to you."

"About?"

"Will you open the door?"

She took another sip of her coffee and thought about it, her wounded ankle suspended in the air.

"No."

"I can't talk to you through the door."

"What's with the unannounced visit? Where's Parkman? How many people do you have with you? Since I don't have any new information for you and I didn't call you, why are you standing outside my door? You see, Mr. Hirst, I have too many unanswered questions to simply open the door. I'm just a little girl with a broken ankle. It's too dangerous to open the door to men I don't really know. Bye-bye."

"You know me," he said. "I'm Parkman's colleague. You can trust me."

She sipped more of the coffee. "Thanks for the advice,

but I decide who I trust, and right now, that's only Parkman. Not after what happened in Canada, anyway. So move away from my door and enjoy the rest of your day. Remember, I'm only here because Parkman asked me to be. I'm not here for you."

She moved back to the desk slowly, making sure not to spill her coffee. Even if Hirst was clean and only here to talk, which she felt most likely, it was rude to just show up at a girl's hotel room unannounced. Especially considering what she went through in Canada. All of North America heard her name in connection with the brutal murder of a police officer. Even though she was cleared, it still changed how cops looked at her.

By the time she finished her first coffee and was getting up to pour more, there was another knock at the door. She hobbled over to it and smacked it hard with her hand.

"Are you thick? Go away. Don't you have something more important to do than harass me?"

"Sarah, it's Parkman."

"Oh, shit." She unlocked the door and opened it. "Sorry. I thought you were Hirst—"

Detective David Hirst stepped into view from the right side of the door. She glared at Parkman.

"What?" He shrugged. "I didn't trick you. He said you wouldn't talk to him without me. I was in the restaurant eating a tasty breakfast. Now I'm here." He walked past her into the room, fiddling with his toothpick. "So talk, Hirst. Tell her what you came to tell her."

"Yeah, tell me what was so bloody important."

Hirst entered the room and closed the door behind him. Sarah headed for the chair at the desk to get off her good foot. She couldn't be mad at Parkman. The opposite, actually. She owed him for almost killing him in Santa Rosa last month. Then he saved her life from a maniacal cannibal in Canada. Being eternally grateful to Parkman meant just that. It also meant she would do anything for him and couldn't wait for the chance to repay him for the sacrifices he had made for her.

On the other hand, she'd just met Hirst and always let the other person set the standard. If Hirst remained respectful, she would be respectful. If Hirst were a dick, she would respond in kind. Friend of Parkman's or not, she had to engage in a relationship with professionals on her terms from the get-go, or it wouldn't work.

Hirst crossed his arms as he leaned back on the room's door.

"My hands are tied," he said. "I don't know what to do or where to go with this case. Calls are being made. Big shots are coming to L.A. If I don't get some leads on this case within a couple of days, they're going to form a task force and take it from me."

"What are you saying?" Sarah asked. "Are we done here?"

"You'll be off the case by the weekend if nothing breaks. Let me rephrase that. I will be off the case this weekend if nothing breaks."

"What big shots are you talking about?" Sarah went to drink from her cup and forgot she hadn't refilled it yet. She got up and started for the kitchenette, but Parkman raised a hand. He took her cup and refilled it for her.

"The Catholic church is bringing in a representative from Rome."

"How does that affect you?" Sarah asked. "Or us? Aren't we only advisors?"

"That's why I'm here." Hirst pushed off the door and walked farther into the room. He addressed Sarah directly. "I've heard about you for years. I knew Parkman was your friend. I have always wanted to meet you. When I got to three dead bodies with no clues, not even DNA under a fingernail, I called Parkman. Well, here you are," he spread his hands wide, "and still, I have nothing."

"There's no guarantees with what I do. I'm sure Parkman was clear on that point."

"Yes." Hirst nodded at Parkman. "Yes, he was." He brought his attention back to Sarah. "Not to mention the flack I'm getting for you being here."

"None of this is my problem. Nor will I feel responsible for it. If I can help, I will. If I can't, well, you get the picture. Is there anything else?"

"There is." Hirst tapped his bottom lip and looked down at the carpet, lost in thought. "Have you ever met Father Adams before?"

"No. Why?"

Hirst met her gaze. "You seemed overly aggressive with him last night."

"It's in my nature." She drank from her cup. "I wish I was softer, kinder." She shrugged. "But I'm not." She offered him a wry smile. Then her lips drew back to a line again. "It's kept me alive."

"Father Adams seemed anxious in your presence."

"Maybe he can recognize when someone isn't intimidated by the clothes he wears or what his belief system is. I don't have a lot of respect for authority, to begin with.

Don't get me wrong. I have no personal issue with religion. Believe in what works for you, and let me believe in what works for me. I would never push my beliefs on anyone, and I don't want to be preached to. But when a man walks around thinking he has an idea of what God might think or say—well, that man is just a clown in vestments. Yeah," she nodded, "that's what he might have felt from me."

"So you two don't have any history?"

She looked at Parkman, then back at Hirst. "Really? Didn't I just answer that?" She turned back to Parkman. "How do you know this guy again?"

"Sarah," Parkman said. "If you don't have anything, I'm fine with that, and so is the detective. Calling us down to L.A. was a last-ditch attempt." Parkman walked over to Hirst, his hand extended. They shook firmly. "I'm sorry we couldn't be more helpful."

"It's fine, really." Hirst looked past Parkman at Sarah. "I believe in what you do because I trust Parkman. He wouldn't bring a charlatan to me. I guess I was just hoping you'd have something."

Hirst released Parkman's hand and stood there, his suit clean and pressed, Windsor-knotted tie, shiny black shoes. He looked like the stereotypical TV detective. The strain showed on his face. He needed to eat better and slow down.

"I have a name," Sarah said.

Both men exchanged glances.

Hirst, his eyebrows raised, said, "A name?"

"Gaspard de Coligny."

"What kind of name is that, and how does it help us here?" Parkman asked.

"Vivian gave me the name when we were called to come

out to the murder scene last night."

"Why didn't you tell us this last night?" Hirst asked.

"The name wasn't relevant last night. It is now."

"How could you know it wasn't relevant last night?"

"Because your killer always engraves the victims' names on a cross. You would know the name of the body regardless of its condition. He has been consistent on that point."

"What if it's the name of the killer?"

"It's not the name of the killer."

"How could you possibly know something like that?"

"Google it. You'll see that Gaspard has been dead for over four hundred years."

"We're really getting nowhere with this, aren't we?" Hirst put his hands on his hips. "How is it relevant at all, then?"

"Your killer isn't just out to execute Catholic priests. He's replicating atrocities the Catholic church has been involved with going back as far as the Crusades and the Inquisition. At least that's my guess."

Hirst and Parkman both frowned. Parkman spoke first.

"You got all that from a name?" he asked.

"Let me ask you something," Sarah said as she placed her coffee cup on the desk beside her computer. She rested her broken foot out in front of her. "The body you found last night, were the clothes wet?"

Hirst's eyes twitched briefly. He was surprised, astonished.

"How … did you know that? It was dark. He was partially covered in dirt. You didn't get down and examine the remains." His voice rose a notch. "How could you possibly know that?"

"Gaspard de Coligny was stabbed with a sword in the 1500s. A mob of Catholics mutilated his body by cutting off his head, extremities, and genitals. Then they dumped him in a river. After a moment's reflection, they decided he wasn't fit for fish food, so they yanked the corpse out of the water and dragged his body to a local gallows where they let the maggots work on him." She waited a moment to let that sink in. "When the call came last night, Vivian gave me the Gaspard name. It's not that hard to figure out the killer is reenacting against the Catholics what the Catholics have done to others. Since the Catholic church has committed hundreds of atrocities over centuries, and your killer is picking them at random for each kill, you won't be able to catch him by that alone. There are simply too many horrors committed by the church over the centuries to nail one down, let alone know what his next murder will copy."

Hirst moved to the bed and sat on the corner. Parkman went to the window and looked out.

"We do crime scene analysis, fingerprints, DNA, investigative work," Hirst said. "I hadn't thought of examining the kill to see if it had been done before." He turned to face her. "I would've never discovered the murder of a man in the 1500s. Even if we did, I would've brushed it off as a coincidence. Father Alvin went through the exact method of murder that you just described."

"This means," Parkman said, "you have an educated man out there killing priests."

"An angry man," Sarah added. "Someone who hates Catholics. Probably someone who has had a terrible experience with them. There has to be something to drive a man to murder priests in a way that resembles past crimes committed by the church. Father Alvin wasn't the only victim killed to replicate the past, I'm sure."

"I didn't tell you everything about the first few victims," Hirst said.

"Now's your chance."

He didn't hesitate. "The first two priests were sodomized. Both had their rectums ruined after death."

Parkman shuddered.

Sarah asked, "Were those the two under suspicion for touching children?"

Hirst nodded.

"Sounds like you have your case. Find a man who has a personal vendetta against the church and is pretty angry at what it's done in the past. When I looked up the Catholic church, the list of horrors committed by it was long. We're talking millions of people killed since the days Jesus walked the Earth. The original crusaders were called the Knights of Christ. The crusades alone cost the lives of over three million people. During the sacking of a German town in the 17th century, over 30,000 Protestants were killed. They found fifty women in one church, beheaded, their infants still sucking their dead mothers' breasts." Sarah shook her head. "I can see how this guy is angry at Catholics. The more I learned, the more I began to despise Catholicism."

The two men remained quiet, taking it all in.

"Maybe that's why my sister isn't really helping," Sarah added.

"How's that?" Hirst asked.

"This guy is only killing priests under suspicion of deviant behavior. He isn't attacking random Catholics. He appears to be a religious vigilante."

"And …"

"Why would Vivian and I, somewhat a vigilante myself, expend too much effort stopping another vigilante from ridding the world of scum?" She raised her hands before either man could say anything. "I'm not saying what he's doing is right. The guy's deranged, and he needs to be stopped. What I am saying is, maybe Vivian will step in before he hurts an innocent." She pulled the note out of her pocket. "She specifically said, 'Everybody and everything has its time.'"

Hirst wiped his face with his hands. Parkman pulled a fresh toothpick out of his pocket and slipped it in his mouth, tossing the old one in the garbage.

"Anyway," Hirst got up off the bed and walked to the door. "I came by to thank you two for coming down, but this thing got too big too fast. Too many dead priests. Sorry to waste your time, but with a task force being put together, we're done here."

"No, no," Parkman said as he walked over to join Hirst at the door. "No waste of time at all. Glad we could come down and take a look at the case. Just sorry we couldn't help you more."

"Sorry, Sarah. Wish we could've solved this together. I'd love to see you in action."

She nodded.

I thought we had until the weekend? What changed?

Something wasn't right, but she couldn't put her finger on it.

Hirst opened the door and stepped into the hallway.

"Detective Hirst?" Sarah said. Parkman held the door open. She had a direct line of sight to him. "Are you under pressure to get rid of the psychic girl? Were you told to send us home?"

Hirst looked unsure how to answer. For such a seasoned detective, she was surprised how much he wore his heart on his sleeve. Something about this decision was tearing him apart. Maybe she would have to dig deeper into the relationship between Hirst and Parkman. What had bonded these two men so deeply?

"No, Sarah." Hirst avoided looking at Parkman. "This is just how it is. There's no case anymore. No need to have you here. Go home. Leave soon."

Leave soon? What the hell does that mean?

"There's still a case," she said.

"It isn't mine. Nor is it yours."

Sarah looked away, the debate pointless. Parkman said goodbye and closed the door. He stood by it a moment, then reopened it.

"I'll go pack my things. Maybe we can get to Santa Rosa by nightfall. You should be resting that foot at home, anyway."

"I'm not going anywhere."

"Sarah, you heard the detective. We're done here."

"I'm not. Everybody and everything has its time. Just like my sister said." She pivoted on her chair and looked at him. "I'm staying until this guy is caught, whether the police like it or not."

"Oh shit, here we go …"

Her hand numbed. She grabbed a pen but couldn't find paper. The white paint on the hotel's wall drew her eye.

She slipped off the chair as her arm numbed, always mindful of her broken ankle, and lunged toward the wall, pen hand first.

She passed out before she made it.

Chapter 4

MIKE STOOD UNDER THE shower too long. His skin had
reddened, and the glass doors had fogged up. He could no
longer see Evelyn on the bed. He shut the water off and slid
the shower door aside.

Eve lay spread out, arms secured above her head, gag in
her mouth. She turned toward him and glared. He smiled
back. There was nothing quite like having someone hate you.
He would have to get used to it. Love was the business of the
church. Hate was his business, despair, and cruelty his
currency. He was Satan's instrument. Hell would offer him
suffering that nothing on Earth could match. Eve's hatred of
him was simply an appetizer of things to come.

Last night was wonderful. After leaving his crime scene,
he had found Eve in the parking lot she usually inhabited on
Sunset Blvd. Mrs. Routine. Seven days a week, she turned
tricks and fed her drug habit. All this at the tender age of

eighteen.

He toweled himself dry and stepped into the bedroom naked.

"You look scared, even frantic, panicky."

Her wide eyes blinked rapidly. Sweat beaded on her forehead as she pulled on the handcuffs that locked her wrists to the bed's metal headboard.

"Withdrawal," he said softly, trying to sound sympathetic. "You're going through withdrawal." He walked around the bed and examined her womanhood. "I'll be busy today. When I'm done and your withdrawal symptoms have minimized, we'll spend the weekend together." He crawled onto the bed, his body hovering over hers, his member dangling down far enough to caress her labia. "We'll have a good time without the effects of drugs. How does that sound?"

She twisted her head back and forth, moaning behind the gag, bucking her hips.

He lifted off her, picked up his clothes, and began to dress.

"No more streets for you, Eve. The rest of your life starts now. I am your savior." He slipped a T-shirt over his head. "The men who offered you security, those pimps you paid, they won't see you again. They'll have to live off the backs of other whores. Trust me. You'll like your new life. It'll be warm, comfortable, and safe. Your new life will be nothing like the streets. And as much sex as I can physically have in a day will be nothing to the ten or fifteen random men you were sleeping with daily. Can't you see? I'm doing you a favor here."

She moaned and kicked her feet.

"It does no good to fight it. Soon enough, you'll be quiet on the inside. You'll sleep. From here on in, we'll be like Adam and Eve in the Garden. Just you and me. Naked. No sin. Unless, of course, you tempt me." He pointed at the large cage that housed his precious beast on the floor in the far corner. "That's an African Rock Python. He's just over twenty feet long and weighs north of one hundred and fifty pounds." He looked back at Eve. "Those things eat monkeys, crocodiles, dogs, goats, pigs, and even deer. I may have to release the snake if you tempt me, as Eve tempted Adam." He spread his hands out wide. "It couldn't be a complete Garden of Eden without the snake, could it?" He lowered his hands to his side. "You're what, a hundred pounds wet? Those things," he pointed at the cage again, "have been known to kill ten-year-olds. I read once that an African Rock could eat a human. You wouldn't want that serpent released while you're tied up. He's seriously hungry. Hasn't eaten in over a month."

Mike grinned and turned away to slip into his shoes. For today's kill, his job was done. The room downstairs was ready. Asbestos lined the walls, and every inch of the room had been sealed. The sulfuric acid sat calmly in its holding tank, almost innocently, and the cyanide pellets awaited their mission. Everything he needed to place Father George into his homemade gas chamber was set up. Within hours, the world would be missing another priest.

At the door, he turned back to Evelyn.

"Be back shortly. Don't go anywhere." He laughed at his own joke.

The look on Eve's face was one of strain and effort. This was good. Suffering was good. It was what Lucifer had asked of him. Cause the most suffering he could and send the vilest to Hell. The first battle that ever occurred was in Heaven when Satan was cast out, and the angel fell. The last battle would occur on Earth with Satan and Mike at the helm.

He closed the door and headed downstairs. The day was rife with possibilities and exciting adventures. Watching Father George die made him feel like a kid again. His parents had been extremely religious. Fundamentally so. They did not spare the rod when they caught him hurting a frog, one of God's creatures. When they caught him reading, they did not spare the rod. And they did not spare the rod when they caught him using the Lord's name in vain.

Mike wouldn't spare the rod either.

Satan's staff was long and barbed, and it spared no one.

Just the way Mike liked it.

Chapter 5

SARAH SNAPPED AWAKE AND shook off the vestiges of her sister's presence. The pen had made marks and indentations across the lower part of the wall. The first word was barely legible, but the second word could be read easily.

"Mercedes?" Sarah asked out loud. "What could Vivian mean? And why not message me when I'm more prepared to take it?" She turned to Parkman. "One day, Vivian will have to let me in on how much freedom she has in offering me information. It would be much better to spell everything out instead of this."

Parkman scanned the message. He knelt and ran his fingers along the wall where the pen had tried to make a mark but missed. He looked at it from the left and then the right. After a moment, he turned the small desk lamp on and moved it to the edge of the desk. The lamp highlighted the rest of the words by casting a shadow where the ink failed.

"Okay," Parkman said. "I'm reading Mercedes, Bing's parking lot. Sunset. 101 2-3. Then there's an A and the start of another letter. You see the same?"

Sarah nodded. "But what's after the A? Another word or just a letter?"

Parkman pointed at her computer. "Do you mind?"

"No, go ahead."

She looked over his shoulder as he typed in a search for Bing's in Los Angeles.

When the screen filled, she asked, "Which one do we go to? There's so many." She stood back and stared at the message on the wall, frustrated. "Vivian, couldn't you be more specific?"

Parkman clicked between the Bing's restaurants on the screen. "Maybe it has something to do with the sunset." He rolled his toothpick to the other side of his mouth.

Sarah's stomach grumbled. She hadn't eaten breakfast yet, and with the talk of Bing's restaurants, she started thinking about eggs and bacon. "Maybe at sunset, we are to go to a Bing's and locate a Mercedes. Could be the killer's car is a Mercedes."

Parkman typed hard on the keyboard. The screen changed again.

For a brief moment, the word *sunset* rolled through her mind as if someone else thought it. Like a part of Vivian's essence lingered in her consciousness. After Vivian had channeled through Sarah's body in the basement of that house in Canada, Sarah felt closer to Vivian. Like they both occupied space under Sarah's skin. It was creepy but, at the same time, welcoming and comforting.

To take over her consciousness and perform her

automatic writing, Vivian already had some kind of control over Sarah. In the past, there had been times when Vivian had manipulated Sarah's muscles. Once she made Sarah trip and fall in Italy, which had saved her life. Channeling messages through Sarah was one thing. Actively taking over Sarah's body was the stuff of horror movies.

Maybe the Catholic church could perform an exorcism on me.

"Parkman, the word sunset has nothing to do with the sun."

"What?"

"Check how many Bing's there are on Sunset Boulevard."

He brought up their webpage and clicked on the store locator link. "Looks like at least two."

"Is there one on Sunset Boulevard near the Hollywood Freeway?"

"Why the Hollywood Freeway?"

"Just look."

After a moment of searching, he turned in his seat and stared at her. "There is."

"The Hollywood Freeway is the 101. See," she pointed at the wall, "the message says Bing's parking lot. Then it says Sunset, and then 101. That's the Bing's we need." She thought about it again while Parkman stared at the wall. "Could the 2-3 with the A after it mean 2:00 to 3:00 am?"

Parkman clapped his hands. "You got it. That's what it looks like it says to me."

"Perfect." Sarah hopped on her good foot until she got to the bed, where she plopped down. "I'm going to get dressed. After that, I want to eat. Then I want to do more research on the Catholic church and take a nap. I'm thinking it'll be a long night."

"What do you expect to find tonight?"

"I have no idea, but I do know we're looking for a Mercedes. Inside that car, we'll probably find the madman Detective Hirst is investigating, or we'll find another body."

"Shit." Parkman got up and walked to the door. "We should be armed."

Sarah nodded. "Can you handle that?"

"I'll try. Hirst'll be no help. We're supposed to be leaving."

"Do your best, Parkman. We need weapons."

He opened the door and exited without another word.

Sarah looked up at the ceiling of the hotel room. "Vivian, you have got to make this easier."

She slipped out of her track pants gingerly, mindful of her broken ankle, feeling every bit a stranger in her own body.

Another presence lingered in her mental shadows. Vivian remained close. So close that Sarah could almost smell her. Like they were twins inhabiting the same body. The only creepy parts were the thoughts and memories that popped up occasionally. Ones that weren't Sarah's. Ones of a different date and time.

An image of her parents had formed in her mind two days ago when her parents were in their twenties. A time before Sarah was born.

Goosebumps accompanied that image. It was impossible for Sarah to have seen her parents, listened to them, or walked with them in those years.

Only Vivian knew Caleb and Amelia then. Only Vivian

had those thoughts and memories.

But why would Vivian's human presence be coming through to Sarah? Could it be due to what happened in Canada when Vivian had completely taken over Sarah's body?

If so, what would happen to Sarah if Vivian did it again? Would she lose more of herself? Could Vivian ultimately take over and lock Sarah out of her body somehow?

She shuddered at the thought.

"Just help me stop this killer, Vivian. Then carry on. Sanity is something I kind of enjoy having."

Sarah was afraid for the first time of what her gift might be doing to her.

Could Vivian's purpose pull Sarah out of depression all those years ago, effectively saving her life, only to kill her on the inside because she had channeled through her too often?

"Only time will tell," she whispered to the empty room.

Chapter 6

Father Adams examined the night stars for a sign from God. When none came, he donned his black hat and gripped the door handle of the church. From just outside the door, he could hear Father George offering a sermon on sin. It was a good sermon. One Father Adams had performed himself over the years. He entered the church, taking pains to remain as silent as possible.

The church had a good crowd, as Father George was popular with the congregation. He was gentle, kind, and good with kids. Perhaps a little too good. Ultimately Father George had been shuffled around the Catholic churches of America until he landed in the big city of Los Angeles under the watchful eye of Father Adams. Today was a day Father Adams dreaded as he needed to give Father George a sermon of his own.

"God is ready to heal those who sincerely wish to amend

their lives," Father George said from the pulpit. "But he won't take pity on the obstinate sinner."

Father George's eyes stopped on Adams. He paused, nodded, and then continued.

"The Lord pardons sins, but he cannot pardon those who are determined to offend him." He raised his hand, pointing skyward. "Nor can we demand from God a reason why he pardons one a hundred sins and takes others out of life and sends them to Hell after three or four sins." He lowered his arm and gripped the sides of the pulpit with both hands. "He who receives pardon, says St. Augustine, is pardoned through the pure mercy of God. They who are chastised are justly punished."

Father Adams leaned against one of the pillars until Father George finished. He watched as the priest walked some of his congregation to the doors and whispered goodbyes to the lot of them. Father Adams involved himself with some of the people filing out of the church and remained patient, as the Lord would expect of a man in his position.

After a time, the big doors shut on the front of the church, with only a few remaining to pray silently.

Father George strode over to address Adams. "To what do I owe the pleasure of this evening's visit?"

"I wanted to have a quick word with you." Adams turned and clasped his hands behind his back. "Walk with me."

When they reached the back of the church, Father Adams pushed open the door of Father George's office. Moments later, they were alone.

"Quite the sermon this evening," Adams said.

"I was pleased with the turnout," George replied. "My

sermon on sin has always been my favorite. Now, Father Adams, what can I help you with?"

Adams stood by the door as George walked around and sat behind his desk.

"As you're probably aware," Adams started, "five of our fellow clergymen have been sent home to God recently."

Father George nodded, a grim expression on his face.

"You might not know that these men were brought here by the Vatican."

"Brought here?" Father George asked, eyebrows raised.

"Shuffled here from other churches in other cities."

"That happens all the time."

"Like in your case, all five were moved here to avoid prosecution or detection."

Father George's expression darkened.

"As you have probably read in the papers, the United Nations slammed the Vatican last February for looking the other way regarding the sexual abuse of children by priests. They demanded the Vatican turn over offenders to face justice. The church official's imposed code of silence, along with moving abusers from church to church, has not been entirely successful." Father Adams remained by the door, his hands comfortably clasped in front of him. "Many bishops involved in these affairs have resigned after abuse scandals in their dioceses, but evidently, it appears someone out there doesn't think that's enough."

"How does this affect me?" Father George asked.

Father Adams wasn't sure whether George had reoffended here in L.A. or not. But he had the dossier on Father George, and he knew what the man had been accused of several times before he was transferred to L.A.

"Based on your alleged history in Pennsylvania and what has happened to those five priests recently, I felt it wise to caution you."

"Are you cautioning others?" Father George asked.

It was easy to see this conversation had made Father George uncomfortable. It probably wasn't something the man wanted to discuss since his past had been buried.

"Look, Father George, I like the work you do here. It's been a year since you arrived, and the people have responded well to you. I just thought you should know."

"Know what?" Father George leaned forward and placed his elbows on the desktop.

"The police are hunting what looks like a serial killer. One that only targets Catholic priests. Every one of these priests had a questionable past concerning the church."

"Are you saying my past is questionable?"

Father Adams wasn't used to being challenged, nor was he accustomed to the aggression he felt coming from Father George. He held his composure, waited a few breaths, then said, "Father George, when you came to me, you were close to being excommunicated. The accusations—"

Father George held up his hand. "That's exactly what they were—accusations. Nothing but faithless lies. A test of my faith. The church saw it my way and transferred me. Father Adams, just because my file has accusations in it, they cannot be verified as they are unproved allegations." He smiled the same wide, calming smile he offered his congregation. "You, of all people, must know that."

"I am simply here in an advisory capacity today. After last night's murder, I felt it necessary to warn the members of our church who have experienced difficulty in the past." He turned and opened the door. "Please wait for me here. I must use the restroom."

Father Adams stepped out into the hallway. Before he got too far, a man walked by, his shoulder bumping Adams.

He turned back but missed the man's face. There was a familiarity in how the man walked and carried himself.

Father Adams turned back around and walked the rest of the way to the restroom.

Chapter 7

MIKE TRIED TO AVOID bumping into the priest, but the hallway was too narrow to accommodate both of them, shoulder to shoulder. At least the priest didn't get a good look at his face.

Father George's office door sat ajar. Mike listened at the door, not wanting to dawdle too long. When he heard no one talking inside, he pushed open the door.

"Father George?" Mike said. "I wonder if I could have a word with you."

Father George sat behind his large desk, a clutter of papers scattered about on top. He leaned back in his chair and nodded.

"Come in."

Mike entered the office until his thighs pressed against the desk.

"As you're aware, Father George, I'm in charge of our recent campaign to locate and renovate shelters within the city limits where we can provide the word of God to the homeless."

Father George nodded but remained silent.

"I wonder if you would like to accompany me to view one of our recent acquisitions. We're renovating an old building. The contractors come in next week, but before they do, I would like your blessing on the choice of building. It would only take an hour. Are you up to it?"

Father George nodded. "It would be a pleasure. But at this late hour?"

"I won't keep you long. I promise."

"Fair enough, Mike. I was in a meeting moments ago, but I think what had to be said was said. I'd be happy to get some fresh air. Let me get my things."

A minute later, Father George, Bible in hand, followed as Mike led them out the back way to his car. Mike started the late-model Pontiac and pushed the cigarette lighter in.

"You smoke?" Father George asked as he slipped his safety belt on. "For some reason, I thought you were allergic to cigarette smoke."

Mike shook his head. "I've been smoking since I was fourteen. You must have me mixed up with someone else."

He pulled out of the church parking lot, careful to make sure no one looked directly at his face.

When they find Father George's body tomorrow, Mike didn't want anyone offering his description to a police sketch artist. Mike was Satan's instrument. Having the police on his tail would only slow his mission, upsetting Lucifer, which Mike didn't want.

But if the authorities got too close, he would sacrifice them because anyone who attempted to stop his mission opposed him.

That meant all opposition had to die.

Even if it was a young girl with a broken foot, who attended his crime scene last night. He now knew exactly who she was and what she was called here to do, and there was nothing he wouldn't do to end her life before she got too close to him.

Young or old, male or female, they were all Lucifer's for the taking.

He would see to it.

Chapter 8

MIKE OPENED THE SIDE door to the building with his key and led Father George through the main floor.

"The city foreclosed on the building, and the church bought it from them for a rather low price," Mike said.

They stopped by one of the bathrooms that were in the process of being torn out. The upstairs still had running water, but Father George wouldn't make it upstairs. Mike didn't want Father George to see Evelyn strapped to the bed. With George's history of molestation, maybe he would want a taste. But Eve was eighteen, probably too old for George.

He guided him toward the small room under Eve's. The sealed room where the sulfuric acid waited. The homemade gas chamber.

"Back here, we have storage rooms that are already finished." He pulled out his key ring and unlocked the door to the last room Father George would ever see. "Inside here, we'll store dry goods for the shelter."

The priest stepped back.

"Father George, what's the matter?"

"Why did you bring me here?" he asked.

Mike held the door open to the room he needed the priest to enter. "I want your opinion on the building. Actually, I want your approval on the project."

"I've never seen you smoke," Father George said as he stepped back once more from the entrance to the store room.

"Is that what this distance between us is all about?"

"No, but you have surprised me a few times today. Your behavior has been unbecoming."

Mike looked down at his polished black shoes. "This has been a very difficult week for me with all the murders—"

"I understand, but—"

"No, let me finish." Mike met his gaze. "In the face of such evil, we have to persevere. We have to continue to do good and be active in the face of evil, always moving forward. The only thing that goes with the flow is dead fish. We can't be dead fish, Father. We have a mission." He cleared his throat. "After this past week, I felt I needed to share this building and the future renovations with you. Since the congregation likes you so much, I thought you might want to prepare a sermon on what we're doing here." Mike waited a moment to let his words sink in. "Let's finish the tour, and then we can discuss your thoughts on it."

Father George nodded, seemingly accepting the explanation, and started for the sealed room.

Something clunked upstairs.

Eve.

Father George looked up at the ceiling. "What was that?"

"I'm not sure," Mike said. He maneuvered himself behind the priest. "I found squatters here a few days ago, and we have running water upstairs." He looked back at George. "Stay here for a minute. I'll go up and take a look."

"I'll go with you."

"No, no. Stay here. I'll be right back."

"Nonsense. I won't have you walking up there alone."

Father George made to pass by him and enter the hallway again. Mike was too close to locking George into the sealed room to let him escape. The door was still wide open. The room beckoned from behind George. This was simply a test. Would he fail Satan or not?

Mike lowered his arm, placed a hand on Father George's chest, and held it there. George looked down at the offending hand. When he glanced up, his mouth was agape, and his eyes were wide.

Mike shoved Father George backward so hard the priest stumbled a few steps before falling on his butt inside the room.

"Enjoy your short stay," Mike said, "at Hotel Hell."

He slammed and locked the door before Father George could get up. As Mike walked away, the priest pounded on the door, his screams muted.

Mike's stomach tightened in anticipation of what would happen next. It would be quite something to watch. If only the church knew how much money Mike had spent setting up his death chambers, how much money he had embezzled from the church to make this building and its unholy fixings a reality, he would spend the rest of his days in jail.

Unless they just sent him to another church to cover it up.

He snickered to himself.

The church had been involved in mass murder for years. How would this be any different?

Another hard clunk reverberated from above.

"I'm coming, Eve," he shouted. "We're going to watch a gas chamber show. But I need to teach you to not interrupt me when I'm busy. You almost got Father George turned around. You're such a naughty young girl. Time for a little penance."

Mike went upstairs, enjoying the anticipation of his evening's duties as a man with each step.

He'd never seen someone executed by toxic gas before.

"Oh, this is going to be fun."

Chapter 9

SARAH OFFERED DIRECTIONS TO Parkman as they drove along Sunset Blvd. As they neared the signs to access The Hollywood Freeway, Sarah saw the Bing's Breakfast Restaurant on the left.

"There it is," she said. "Pull into the back parking area."

She checked the clock on the dash: 1:55 a.m.

"Once we park, I'll look around for a Mercedes."

"You sure you want to do that with one foot?" Parkman asked. He angled into a parking spot in reverse. "I should do the walking around and searching stuff." He turned off the car and pulled out the keys. "I've got two good legs." He smiled at her.

"I've got two good legs, too," she said.

"Okay, ankle, foot, whatever." Parkman touched the door handle, but Sarah grabbed his other arm.

"Let me," she said. "I can't just sit in the car. I need to

stay active. That's who I am."

He released the door handle and nodded.

Sarah scanned the parking lot. "No Mercedes in this area."

"Heard anything from Vivian? Any idea why we're here looking for a Mercedes?"

Sarah shook her head. "Nothing." She went to open the door but stopped. "Did you turn off the interior light?"

"Yes."

"Good." She pushed open the door, set her good foot on the ground, and pulled her crutch out of the backseat. "I'll be back in a few minutes."

"Sorry, I couldn't get a better weapon," Parkman said. "I tried."

She turned to look at him. The parking lot lights lit up half his face.

"The weapon is fine." She glanced at the hammer on the car floor. He couldn't get a gun. The army surplus store was sold out of pepper spray. Short of buying knives or a scythe, Parkman thought two hammers from the hardware store would have to do. Sarah was no stranger to hammers. She'd used them before to save her life. "There's just no place for me to hide it." She offered him a reassuring smile. "If there's trouble, I'll use my crutch."

"Fair enough. Just scream if you need me. I'll bring my hammer."

"Parkman?"

"Yeah?"

"You sound like Thor." She stepped away from the door and leaned on her crutch. "I'll be okay. Chances are, I won't scream."

"I know."

For two in the morning, the breakfast spot was busy. Over a dozen cars were parked in the lot. A couple walked by on the sidewalk. A man exited his vehicle and headed toward the restaurant. With the area this busy, it was smart of Bing's to stay open all night.

Why am I here, Vivian?

A woman in a short mini-skirt walked alone through a darker part of the lot. She passed the last car and kept walking. She stepped through a small opening in the bushes near the back and disappeared.

That's interesting. And not very safe.

Sarah hobbled along on the crutch until she made it to the sidewalk of Sunset Boulevard. Two girls stood talking out front by a bench at the bus stop. The brunette wore a bikini top and Daisy Duke shorts, while the blonde sported a mini-skirt and a tube top too small to cover her breast implants.

What's with the mini-skirts tonight?

Once the brunette noticed her staring, they stopped talking and turned to face her.

Either a sexy costume party just let out somewhere, or streetwalkers roamed this area of Sunset Boulevard.

"What choo lookin' at?" the brunette asked with a drunken slur.

Sarah started toward them. The brunette snickered as she passed them. Sarah had seen it a hundred times. The posing. The acting tough. It almost made her smile, but she resisted. It was an illusion people fed themselves to feel safe.

"That's right," the blonde said. "You keep strutting your shit. I got it, I got it. You would think it a bit much … to have a lonely customer touch … the stupid girl with a crutch." She laughed as the other girl chimed in on the improv sidewalk rap.

"Stupid girl with a crutch." A slap cracked the air behind Sarah. "That's a riot. Stupid girl. Good one, Stevie."

Sarah stopped walking. She was five or six steps away from them now.

They quieted behind her. She pivoted on the crutch until she faced them.

"Wha' choo gonna do, bitch?" the brunette asked, taking a step forward. "We're working here. It ain't good you walking around out here on a crutch. Bitch, you bad for business."

"Why did she call you Stevie?" Sarah asked. "That your real name?"

They looked at each other. The brunette wrapped an arm around the blonde and leaned into her.

"Girl, you got no idea where you are. Go home to mommy. Go snuggle up safely in your bed. This ain't no place for little orphan Annabelle and her broken foot."

"Ankle."

"What?"

"And my name's not Annabelle."

A car raced by. The door to the restaurant opened, and two men came out, one laughing at something the other said.

Then two names popped into Sarah's head. They came out of nowhere and everywhere. It wasn't an original thought. More like someone planted it there. Just like those internal thoughts after she was shot in the head in Toronto.

Vivian?

"You gonna stand there all night and admire the inventory?" the blonde asked.

"Jessica Fremont and Vicky Chard." The names came with an urgency. Like they were meant to be spoken. Both girls reacted as if punched. The blonde reeled back a step, her fake breasts not moving an inch. The brunette's face displayed shock, but she challenged Sarah by stepping forward.

"You 5-0? You the cops? How you know our names?"

Sarah was hardly ever surprised. A feeling of lightheadedness accompanied the names. Perplexed, she stared at the two girls at the bus stop for a moment too long.

The blonde pulled out a cell phone and dialed a number. The brunette took another step forward as the blonde whispered into her phone.

"If Stevie isn't your name," Sarah said, "and you all go by a street name, then I'm looking for a girl named Mercedes."

It all made sense. The message was specific. Sarah was at the right place, at the right time, searching for a Mercedes. But not a car. A hooker named Mercedes.

She had to tell Parkman. She needed to get back to the car.

"Where's Mercedes?" Sarah tried again.

"No Mercedes here," Brunette said. "What's your business with her?"

"None of yours."

"What?"

"Whatever."

Sarah stepped forward, placed the crutch on the sidewalk, and hopped ahead. As she passed the brunette, she wondered if Vicky would get aggressive, then thought she probably would and prepared for it.

She was right.

Vicky's hands came up to shove Sarah, but she stopped and spun around on the heel of her right foot. When Vicky's hands came in contact with Sarah's right shoulder, Sarah was already spinning and deflected the hands. With nothing to stop or counter her, Vicky's forward motion caused her to fall. She had stepped into it too far. The brunette's heel on her six-inch pumps twisted, and she dropped to one knee.

Sarah finished her spin by coming all the way around, facing forward again, the brunette on one knee in front of her. With a gentle nudge, she pushed Vicky over.

Jessica glanced up from her phone. "What the hell did you do?"

Sarah didn't want the fight. She needed to get back to Parkman.

"You better get over here fast," Jessica said into the phone as she stepped back to give Sarah a wide berth as she passed. "This crazy bitch with a crutch just laid Stevie out on her ass. Stevie's bleeding and shit, man."

Sarah picked up her pace while Jessica talked behind her.

"Bring everyone. I saw this bitch pull in with a guy. They're probably cops."

Sarah turned into the parking area and started toward Parkman in the rental. If both feet were good, Sarah would've knocked the phone out of Jessica's hand, stepped on it, and avoided her backup arriving by at least five to ten minutes.

Maybe they would leave and come back another night. But the place would be too hot, crawling with pimps and backup for weeks until she showed her face again. And why were streetwalkers in the parking lot of a breakfast joint in the middle of the night, anyway?

What the hell, Vivian? Could've given me a heads-up.

Parkman opened the door and got out as she neared the car.

"Did you find the Mercedes?"

"It's not a car," Sarah said. "It's a woman."

Parkman frowned. He had one hand on the roof of the rental and one on the top of the open door.

"A woman?" he asked. "How is a Mercedes a woman?"

"A hooker. It's her stage name or whatever they call it." Sarah stopped at the hood of the car and leaned on it to catch her breath. "Whoever Mercedes is, we need to find her. I suspect we'll discover why when we locate her."

Jessica still watched them from the sidewalk by the street.

"What's with her?" Parkman asked.

"Nothing, really. She got freaked out when Vicky tried to push me."

Parkman snapped his head around. "What? Tried to push you?" He closed the car door and moved closer to her. "You okay?"

"Parkman, I'm fine. I can take care of myself."

"Well, I know that, but your foot."

"Ankle."

He grunted. "Sarah, seriously. We're supposed to be leaving L.A. You should be at home, your foot in the air—I'm sorry—ankle in the air, drinking wine or something. Not out here hunting priest killers and tracking down a prostitute named Mercedes."

"Parkman, I wouldn't want to be anywhere else."

Sarah turned to watch Jessica, but she was gone. The

parking lot was suddenly quiet, with only the distant hum of the Hollywood Freeway.

"What's going on?" Parkman asked.

"No idea, but I think someone knows we're here."

"Someone who?"

"Someone who employs Jessica and Vicky."

Parkman turned to her. "You got their names?"

She pushed off the hood of the car and got to her feet. "Yeah, I guess so. In a way."

"In a way?"

"I think Vivian whispered it to me."

"However you explain it, Sarah, that's amazing. You know that?"

"Don't tell anybody," she whispered with half a smile. "I'll deny the whole thing."

Bushes rattled seven cars down. A tall man stepped out from the same spot where the girl in the mini-skirt had disappeared earlier. As he headed toward Sarah and Parkman, another man emerged from the bushes behind him. Then another.

"Parkman, we may have a problem."

"I see that."

The three men formed a line. All three wore chains that glistened in the streetlights. Gold watches, rings, and even the teeth of the tallest man reflected the light. Pimps in their classic attire. Hoodlums and street gangs were all the same after a while. The kind of people that made others stay home at night but didn't intimidate Sarah. They only made her want to bring their ego down a notch with a broken nose or worse. A gang or not, pain didn't discriminate. The only difference was a man's pain tolerance; when it came down to it, most men hated the dentist.

Sarah scanned the rest of the parking lot for others. Parkman stepped back and opened his car door. He was probably going for the hammer.

"Don't," the tall one shouted. "Just don't."

Parkman froze. Light reflected off the handgun in one man's hand. As the threesome advanced, it became clear all three had handguns out and ready.

Sarah glanced over her shoulder. Neither Jessica nor Vicky was in sight.

"What now?" Parkman whispered. "We can't fight guns with hammers."

"Just be cool. They won't shoot us because one of their girls fell down."

At least, I hope not.

"They probably just want to check us out," Parkman agreed. "If it gets bad fast, I'll drop in the car and speed dial 911."

"Like we need more police attention."

The men stopped a few feet in front of Sarah. The tall one, clearly in charge, stared at her up and down, his mouth drawn back in a snarl, his pearly whites shining through with one gold cap. His black hat covered his ears, his white T-shirt was two sizes too big, and his jeans were hanging low off the waist. His two minions wore similar clothes. The forehead of the guy on her left had street tattoos like the ones she'd seen in Toronto on a street gang.

There was no question these three were street fighters. They were strong and ready to fight in seconds, but the rest was for show. They wanted to ensure everyone knew whose territory this was and who owned the girls.

"You here looking for work?" the tall one asked. The expression on his face told her he already knew the answer.

Miles Johnson.

Sarah shook her head to clear the voice.

What the hell?

She looked around as if someone was whispering in her ear. Parkman was still by the car door. Sarah stood by the car's hood, exposed and at a disadvantage.

"I hope your pretty little ass is here looking for work because if you're not, why the fuck you be up in here messin' around with my girls?"

"You got it wrong, Miles."

He looked at his backup and then at Sarah. "How you know my name?" He clicked something on his gun, then let it fall back to his side. "I asked you a question. Who the fuck are you, and how do you know my name?"

"Where's Mercedes? Stevie didn't want to tell me where she was. If I don't know in"—Sarah pulled back her sleeve and looked at her watch—"five minutes"—she let her sleeve fall back into place—"more people are going to get hurt, just like Stevie."

"Get a load of this bitch," Miles said as he laughed for his friends' benefit. The laugh stopped abruptly. His face turned serious.

Then he rushed her.

She detected Parkman jumping as Miles reached around to grab her hair with his left hand while jamming the tip of the gun under her chin with his right hand. With her head angled back, she looked down her nose at the other two men. Both had their weapons aimed in Parkman's direction.

There was no more movement behind her.

"I love it when a stupid whore talks back to me," Miles said, an inch from her face.

She could smell the burrito he had eaten for dinner. Too much guacamole, she almost said to him.

"It reminds me," Miles continued, "of my past when I would beat my mother for being such a stupid whore."

His grip tightened on her hair, the sharp pain reminding her of the days when she would pull her own hair out. There was something about getting her hair pulled that would always feel comforting, even through the pain.

She raised both hands, so they were level with his gun hand.

"Be cool," she said. "I was just clowning around."

"What you want with Mercedes? Stupid bitch didn't come to work tonight. You have something to do with that?"

"No."

"Then why you here?"

"We wanted Mercedes for a three-way."

His hand tightened on her hair as he smiled.

"I hate liars. If that was true, why attack Stevie? Why go after my girls?"

"I didn't. But that doesn't matter because you've already made up your mind."

"That's right."

His hand tightened again. Her eyes watered. Now it was bordering on serious pain. This was no longer fun.

"Be cool," Sarah said, "or I will break your nose."

An M1911. The slide stop can be depressed from the reverse side to incapacitate the weapon.

Sarah knew enough about guns to know exactly what that meant. No longer flustered by the foreign thoughts, she stared at the gun below her face and saw the slide stop on the side of its barrel, right above the grip.

Miles talked through his teeth. "I got the gun on you, and you want to threaten me?" He laughed deep in his throat.

Cars approached. Tires screeched. Maybe the police had arrived. Maybe someone inside the restaurant had called them.

"I think it's time to teach bitch girl here a lesson." Miles released her hair.

With her left hand, Sarah grabbed Miles's gun wrist, shoved the gun a few degrees up and to the left, away from her and Parkman, and dropped her head the opposite way. As her right hand grabbed the top of the gun to jam the slide back, the gun fired.

Chapter 10

WHEN MIKE ENTERED THE room, Evelyn was right where he'd left her. Only this time, her wrists were bleeding.

"What have you been up to?" he asked.

She grunted, the gag held firmly in place by the duct tape wrapped around her head. She would have to pull out her hair to remove the gag.

"You've been hurting yourself with those cuffs." He looked at her sidelong and pointed. "You've been a bad girl." He spread his hands wide. "Where's the gratitude? I pulled you away from that disgusting, vile life." He moved to the end of the bed. "No more dealing with pimps. No more random men with their random cocks. Only me until we both die in the explosion."

Eve bucked on the bed and screamed behind the gag, which came out as a deep-throated moan.

"Oh, I forgot to tell you that part." He pulled the

handcuff key out of his pocket and released the cuffs from the metal headboard. "The fastest way to hell is through fire. Once you're already burning, it doesn't hurt as much when you fall into the lake of fire. And since I'm Satan's chosen one, which means I'll be stoking the flames throughout Hell, I want to get used to burning."

Evelyn's eyes widened. She pulled away and curled into a ball. The cuffs dangled from her wrists, but she did not attempt to escape.

"Because you're my sacrifice, you must burn with me." He stepped away from the bed and stopped in the doorway. "It'll be okay. You'll enjoy Hell. The explosion will be quick, then boom, there we are. It'll be like taking an express elevator to Hell."

Evelyn cried, her shoulders hitching with sobs.

"Oh, come on. It isn't so bad." He stomped the floor twice to get her attention. "Come downstairs. We'll cut a hole in your gag and get you something to eat. But first, I have a surprise for you."

She stayed on the bed, naked, whimpering.

"Eve, get up and come with me. Do as I say. You know I won't spare the rod." She moved, but not fast enough. "If you don't get up right now, I will hurt you so bad you won't be able to walk for a week. Do you understand me?"

She nodded subtly. Her body unraveled, and she straightened out on the bed.

"We haven't got time for this. Get up now and come to my side."

Eve sat up and wiped her face with her hands, the cuffs bumping her cheeks. She got to her feet, wobbled, caught herself, and started around the bed toward him. He waited.

He slapped her face when she was two feet in front of him.

She went down as the slap sucked the life out of her legs. He grabbed a wad of her hair and lifted it. She screamed behind the gag, her breasts bobbing as she shuddered under his grasp.

Eve's pain and suffering delighted him. It reminded him of his youth, his parents, and all the torture he endured under their hands, their rods that weren't spared. In a curious way, hurting someone else was a form of release.

When he got her up, and on her own feet again, he released her hair.

"You haven't eaten since I brought you here, have you?"

Her glazed, bloodshot eyes found him. She was afraid to answer.

"That's right. You've been gagged because we have neighbors. Couldn't allow you to call for help." He shoved her through the door. "Follow me downstairs for my surprise, and then I will get you something to eat."

She managed the stairs relatively well, leaning into the railing until she reached the bottom, where she stopped walking and used the wall to stay upright.

Mike stepped around her and led the way down the corridor to the next stairwell. He looked back once. She stayed close behind him, her naked form tight, sinewy.

A floor below, at the small window he installed in the wall, Mike looked in at Father George. The man was kneeling in the center of the room, a rosary wrapped around his clasped hands, head tilted back, praying.

Mike slammed the wall and yelled, "Where's your God now? You think whispering words and looking skyward will save you?" Mike roared with laughter. "If there really is a

God, I would love to see him." He turned to Eve. "Do you believe in God?"

She shook her head.

"Good girl. Smart girl." Back at the window, George was on his feet. He mouthed something, but the room was too sealed to hear him.

"What's that?" Mike shouted.

Father George's mouth moved, but nothing came out.

"To hell with you, George." He pointed to a small lever in the wall beside Eve. "Push that down, will you?"

Eve complied.

Mike pressed his face against the glass and watched as dense smoke emitted from the vent on the wall.

Eve stepped closer and peeked inside the room, too. She frowned when she saw Father George.

"Let me explain," Mike said. Eve's pleading eyes met his. "This room is sealed off, and the walls are lined with asbestos. Encased inside the room, I filled a holding tank with concentrated sulfuric acid. That lever you just pushed," he pointed at it again, "released cyanide pellets into the sulfuric acid, which turns it into hydrogen cyanide gas. Basically, it's an asphyxiant gas, similar to the kind used in the chambers where they gassed people during World War II."

Eve's forehead glistened, and her eyes widened as she struggled with what he was telling her. She peeked through the small window again. Mike followed her gaze.

Father George held his throat, his mouth wide, gasping for a clean breath.

"Take a couple of large breaths, Father George. Get that gas deep inside. You'll die faster and avoid a painful, prolonged death. Hurry up the process." Mike looked at his watch.

Eve looked away. She gagged as she bumped into the wall.

"Hey, take it easy. Don't you go throwing up on me."

Mike took one last look at Father George. He had moved to the vent in the wall. He ripped at the homemade seal around it, even as his body convulsed with death.

"Nooo," Mike yelled. "Leave that alone."

If the seal broke, some of the toxic gas would enter the corridor. He would need an oxygen mask to survive. But the only oxygen mask he had was in his van at the rear of the building.

Father George's body bucked and kicked as the gas took over.

Eve gagged behind her sealed-off mouth.

Everything was coming apart too fast, unraveling. He needed Eve to finish his mission. Eve was there at the beginning of the Garden of Eden with Adam, and he needed Eve to be there at the end.

Father George was still now, the contortions over, life finished, death accomplished.

Mike grabbed Eve and slapped her. Her bladder released, and the strong scent of urine filled the hallway. She was devolving in front of him, her throat convulsing.

The only way to save her was to get the duct tape off her mouth. He grabbed it around the back of her neck and pulled it. Eve moaned louder than at any other time before. None of the tape came away, only hair.

He pulled again but only succeeded in lifting Eve a couple of feet.

Everything he had worked for with Eve, the risks he had taken, and the money spent on her unraveled as she vomited in her mouth repeatedly.

"No, no, no …"

Her cheeks distended as her mouth filled with bile with nowhere to go. As her stomach clenched and more vomit shot upward, Eve could not swallow it back in time. As she choked on her own liquids, he released her. She dropped to the floor in a fit of seizures, and her eyes rolled back in her head.

Tan-colored stomach contents spilled out her nostrils, cutting off all airways, and after another seizure, she stilled on the floor at his feet.

"Mother Mary! Now what?"

He wouldn't have brought her down for it if he had known she would throw up at the sight of Father George's death.

"Dammit."

He kicked her naked corpse.

"What a waste. I was just thinking we could have more fun before the fireworks later."

He looked in at Father George's body. It didn't appear that George succeeded in breaking the seal on the vent, but it was hard to tell as the interior was mostly filled with the white gas.

Mike made up his mind. He was not vacating this building without his African Rock Python. He would take Eve upstairs for one more bout of lovemaking while she was still warm and then leave her to rot.

Instead of pulling her upstairs by her hands and being too close to her putrid vomit, he grabbed her ankles.

"I'm so sorry you had to die like this. I had much better plans for you."

On each stair, her head bounced with a thud. Vomit dripped from her nose, leaving a grotesque trail, a reminder of his mistake.

"This is all because of the Catholics. I had to do this because of what the Catholics did in Croatia." He spoke to Eve as if she could still hear him. "Back in the forties, a man named Anton, a practicing Catholic and regular visitor to the Vatican, ran several extermination camps. One of them was headed by a Franciscan friar. They were called the Catholic Ustashi." At the top of the stairs, he paused and looked back. "Are you listening?" After not getting a response, he started up the last set of stairs dragging Eve's body behind him.

"The Catholic Ustashi burned their victims alive." He glanced back again. "It's a true story. I wouldn't lie to you. That's why Father George had to die this way. You understand, don't you? The eye-for-an-eye thing, live by the sword, die by the sword, doesn't work for humans and God. But it works great for my boss. In the end, he just gets more souls."

When he got to the bedroom, he dragged her body over to the bed, where he set her feet down. Careful to keep her vomit-leaking head near the pillow area where he wouldn't spend much time, he lifted her front half first, then her feet up. He pulled her feet to the end and spread her legs wide. Her neck was craned in an odd position, but that didn't matter. He had no use for the upper part of her body. The urine glistening along her inner thighs aroused him.

He began to undress.

"Have you ever heard of Herman Mudgett?"

Eve didn't respond.

"I didn't think so. His other name was Dr. Henry Howard Holmes. He's referred to as America's first serial killer. In Chicago, he built a huge mansion, which he called 'The Castle.'"

Mike had his pants off and worked on the buttons of his shirt.

"Inside this mansion, there were trap doors, secret passageways, fake walls, and hidden staircases." He held up a finger. "But here's the best part. He lined rooms with asbestos to turn them into homemade gas chambers." Mike removed his underwear. "He was my inspiration for what happened to Father George."

Mike crawled onto the bed. Then he pulled on Eve's hips, raising her buttocks to suit him better. Her skin was clammy and already cool to the touch. He would have to hurry, or she would get too cold too fast for his liking.

"Good old Herman was accredited for twenty-seven murders, but they think there were many more." He stroked his member until he was ready. "I want to beat that number. That really turns me on. To be known for such atrocities does wonders for self-esteem. Counting you, I now have seven deaths at my hand. Seven, count them."

He leaned in closer, ready for her now.

"I should reach ten before I do the rest in one explosion. Wouldn't that be wonderful? One big bang, just like how the Earth started. One big bang and twenty or thirty people will be executed at once. Maybe more, if I can pack them in."

He touched her cool skin with his member.

"Just like right now. One big bang, and you're done." He laughed. "I'll be done, too."

As he entered her corpse, the snake rattled its cage in the corner.

Chapter 11

The deafening report of Miles's gun beside Sarah's face didn't slow her down. Her right hand shoved the slide back and clicked the slide stop into position, all in one fluid motion. The gun was immobilized.

Sarah snapped down at the base of Miles's forearm and twisted his wrist back as far as it would go.

He yelped at the sudden sharp pain, and his grip opened.

In her peripheral vision, she picked up movement behind Miles. His friends were moving in.

The M1911 dropped out of his hand and into hers. With her butt still firmly planted on the hood of the car, she kicked him away with her good foot, dropped the slide stop back into place, slipped her finger inside the trigger guard, aimed, and fired.

The first bullet went wide. She fired again, hitting the face-tattoo man in the calf. Miles made a break for the bushes.

"Freeze," Sarah shouted.

She fired twice into the pavement by his feet, which stopped him, his hands in the air.

A car squealed to a stop nearby. Doors opened.

"Drop the weapon!" someone shouted behind her.

"Identify yourselves," Sarah yelled back without taking her eyes off Miles.

Someone whispered, "You gotta be kidding me."

"We're the Los Angeles Police. Drop the fucking weapon. Now!"

The third gangbanger had disappeared in the bushes. Miles faced away with his hands up. His tattooed friend writhed on the ground holding his leg, a tight expression of pain on his face.

Sarah released the gun handle and let it dangle with her finger inside the trigger guard. Then she lowered it slowly and let it go when it was a foot from the pavement.

The cops moved in fast. One of the officers kicked the gun under Parkman's rental. He grabbed Sarah from behind and yanked her arms back.

"What the hell do you think you're doing?" the cop yelled in her ear. "You just shot that guy in the leg."

"Officer," Parkman said. "Take it easy. That's not how it happened."

The cop turned around. "Stay back there by the car door. You'll get your turn. Keep your hands in the air."

More cruisers pulled in. Two other cops cuffed Miles's wrists. He cried out when they grabbed the wrist Sarah had wrenched. Two paramedics ran for the guy on the ground.

The cop picked up Sarah's crutch and helped her to her

feet. He attempted to support her, but she leaned into him too much with her hands cuffed behind her back and no weight on the crutch.

"Shit," Sarah said. "This isn't going to work—"

As she started to fall, the cop stepped away. All she could think to do was protect her broken ankle. She lifted it high in the second it took to smash her right shoulder into the concrete. The grunt that escaped her lips couldn't be helped. The wind was knocked from her lungs. As she coughed and struggled to breathe again, Vicky stepped into view, a smile from ear to ear on her face.

"How does it feel?" she asked.

Sarah's response was another cough.

"I'm Officer Vicky Chard." She leaned down close to Sarah. "How did you know my name? I've been working undercover for a long time, nailing deadbeat johns. But this operation was for Miles Johnson. Then you walk up, name me, and shoot at my suspect with his own gun. Who the hell are you?"

Sarah caught her breath, but her shoulder ached from the hit. She rested her cast on the concrete and laid her head back. She had no idea how she knew Jessica's or Vicky's names or how to disarm Miles's gun. It was all Vivian's doing. But if so, why still give messages through automatic writing? Why not just talk directly inside her head?

"Why did you grab Miles's gun?" Vicky asked. "You paramilitary trained or something?"

"She just knows stuff," Parkman said. "That's Sarah Roberts."

Vicky straightened up and turned to face Parkman.

"That would make you her colleague, Parkman?"

"You know us?"

"We all heard she was in town. Most of us steered clear for fear of hurting her by accident." Vicky looked back at Sarah. "Your reputation with the authorities precedes you."

The cop who had let her fall came back over. "Oh, are you Sarah Roberts?" he asked, mock surprise on his face. He placed a hand on each cheek, his mouth a gaping hole. "I'm so sorry. I had no idea." He got down and removed the cuffs.

Detective Hirst had kept them isolated from the local cops in case some of them got the wrong idea about her. But now Hirst was nowhere around.

"Can I help her up?" Parkman asked.

Vicky nodded and stepped back to give him room. He slipped both hands under her arms and lifted her back onto the hood of the car.

"You okay?" he asked.

Miles was escorted to a waiting cruiser. He had fired his weapon inches from her face. There had to be attempted murder charges waiting for him. The other guy was on a stretcher being wheeled to a waiting ambulance.

"That was fast," Sarah said, having caught her breath.

"What was?" Vicky asked.

"Your response time." Sarah turned to her. "Everyone was waiting around the corner." Knowing she was right, Sarah continued. "You were planning a bust tonight, but not for the johns. That's the reason for so many cops and an ambulance."

"Why are you here?" Vicky asked. "Was it just to find Mercedes?"

"Would you believe me if I told you?"

"Try me."

"Then yes, we just wanted to talk to Mercedes."

"Weren't you working with homicide on the priest killings?" Vicky asked.

"You know a lot."

Vicky turned to the officer who let Sarah fall. "Hey, Russ, I got this. Go ahead, and I'll meet you downtown."

Russ grunted and turned away, the smile never leaving his face.

"Come have a coffee with me," Vicky said. "We'll talk about Mercedes."

Parkman moved in to help Sarah, but she waved him off, pulled the crutch under her shoulder, and started for the breakfast restaurant.

With Vicky a few steps ahead, Parkman asked, "What's happening, Sarah? How are you getting all their names? How did you know to do that to the gun?"

"I'm not really sure. But whatever it is, I'm loving it."

She caught him staring at her.

"Are you saying you did not have foreknowledge of that gun?"

"Yes, that's what I'm saying. But if Vivian wants to keep planting stuff in my head when I need it, I don't mind. Miles entered that parking lot with intent tonight. Without Vivian, I might have gotten hurt."

Vicky turned around. "Did I hear you say you *might* have gotten hurt with Miles?"

Sarah nodded.

"The last girl he hurt is still in the hospital. We suspect he's killed a few. When I saw him pull the gun on you, I didn't approach until backup arrived." She stared hard at Sarah. "He intended to kill you or, at the very least, maim you."

"Great. Thanks. I feel so much better knowing how close he came."

Vicky reached the restaurant's door and opened it for Sarah. Once they were seated and had ordered coffee, Sarah asked about Mercedes.

"Before I answer," Vicky said, "what's your interest?"

A police cruiser pulled out, the lights reflecting off the restaurant's window. Sarah wondered why no one offered Vicky a jacket to cover up. Maybe she'd been doing this so long that she was comfortable being half exposed.

"We're not sure yet, but we think Mercedes is involved or knows about the priest killings."

"What kind of knowledge?" Vicky asked.

"No idea." Sarah smiled. "Gotta ask her."

"Are you being smart with me?"

"I'm looking for Mercedes. You ask me what kind of knowledge. Until I ask Mercedes, I have no idea what she knows or doesn't know. So no, I'm not being smart with you."

"Mercedes works for Miles. She works till dawn every night in this parking lot after midnight. The only nights she's not here is when Miles lets her stay a whole night with one guy."

"And she's not here tonight," Parkman said.

Vicky shook her head and looked down at a busted nail on her finger. She pulled on it for a second, then met Sarah's eyes.

"Mercedes might be in trouble."

"How so?"

"There's a guy who's been coming around lately. Big

guy. Loads of cash. Takes her for the night. She comes back with handcuff marks on her wrists. I'm worried for her, but Miles doesn't care. As long as he gets his cut."

"When was the last time you saw her?" Parkman asked.

"Two nights ago. She wasn't here last night, either."

The waitress set three cups of coffee in front of them. "Will there be anything else?"

Vicky shook her head. "No thanks."

The waitress walked away as Sarah pulled the cup to her lips and sniffed the aroma before sipping.

"No cream or sugar?" Vicky asked.

"None."

"Me too." After a sip from her cup, Vicky said, "I think Mercedes is afraid of her customer. At least that's what some of the girls were saying."

"How so? Did you hear why?"

"No."

"Have you seen this guy?" Parkman asked. "Can you give us a description?"

"I can do you one better. I followed her two nights ago to see where the client was taking her."

Sarah sat up in her seat. "Really? Take us there."

"I think he detected the tail. I lost them a few blocks from where he lives."

"How do you know you were close to where he lives? You could've lost them before they jumped in a car and drove to the other side of the city."

"He was pulling out his house keys when he noticed me. After putting the keys away, they kept walking. After two blocks and a couple of fast turns, they disappeared."

"Then take us to where you lost them. Walk us the exact

route."

"You can walk that far on a crutch?"

"Don't worry about me. Mercedes's life may be in danger. And if she's involved with the priest killer in any way, if we don't find her, more priests will die."

"Do you know her real name?" Parkman asked.

Vicky lifted her coffee with both hands and said, "Evelyn Wynn. Her name is Evelyn, but the client always calls her Eve."

Chapter 12

Outside the restaurant, Vicky followed them to their rental. The authorities had cleared out of the parking lot already.

"Your team works fast," Sarah said.

"We already had the list of charges prepared as we were set to arrest Miles and his crew tonight. I was talking to Jessica when you walked by us. I was about to pop the question to her."

"Pop the question?" Parkman asked.

"If she would testify against Miles. If not, I would have arrested her out front, away from his sight. My backup was minutes away, as you now know."

"Probably a good night for us to come," Sarah said.

"Sarah?" Vicky stepped closer. "I have to ask. What possessed you to grab Miles's gun? That was either the bravest thing I have ever seen or the stupidest."

"Consider it the stupidest then," Sarah said as she made her way around to the passenger side of the rental. "We'll follow you."

She opened the door and dropped into the seat, the stress of the evening wearing her down. Parkman said a few more words to Vicky and got in the car. He put the keys in the ignition and stopped.

"Sarah, why *did* you grab the gun?"

"He was going to shoot. Didn't want it touching me anymore. Also, I thought I detected a little orange around the barrel. There was a possibility it was fake."

"All guns are real and loaded when they're aimed at you. That's the only rule to live by, literally, the only way to stay alive."

"I know," Sarah said. "Look, Vicky's pulling out. Let's go."

Parkman started the car and pulled out to follow Vicky.

"You handled it expertly," Parkman said. "Any chance there's more you're not telling me? Like how you knew Miles's name."

"I just knew."

"What does that mean?"

She turned to him. "It's Vivian. She talks to me. In my head."

"What?" He glanced at her, then back at the road. "How?"

"She drops words into my consciousness. The handwritten messages tell the future. But at the moment, when I need something new, Vivian speaks to me in the here and now. The words form in my mind, and I can tell they're not my own."

"How long has she been doing this?"

"Since I took that bullet in the head in Toronto." Sarah adjusted her broken foot and rested her arm on the back of the seat. "Vivian has always had control of my body. That's how automatic writing works. She takes over, channeling through me to write messages. Back in Kelowna, she took over my drugged body and fought back when I couldn't. For a time, she actually possessed me."

"I remember you telling me about that."

"But there's a problem with it."

"What's that?" Parkman asked as he slowed the car. Vicky had pulled off Sunset Boulevard and was parking on a side road.

"It feels like there are two people inside my head now. It's weird. Like sometimes I'm the guest."

"And?" Parkman stopped the car and cut the lights. He turned to face her.

"I can feel Vivian's thoughts. Even see some of her memories. It worries me."

"How?"

"Just recently, I saw an image of my parents as if it was a memory. But it couldn't have been my memory as Mom and Dad were too young."

"If that's the only side effect, what does it matter? You rattled Miles and disarmed him because of what Vivian said. That may have saved your life."

"Vivian told me the kind of gun it was and how to disarm it. Mentally, she made it feel like I always knew the M1911 model."

"There you go. Saving your life tonight far outweighs a few memories of Vivian's past."

"Normally, I would agree. But Vivian was raped and murdered at a young age. When those memories surface, what then? How can I cope with that kind of memory when it isn't mine? Parkman, I can handle a lot, but that would ruin me. I can't imagine walking around with a memory of that kind of violation. She died. That would come along with it. Because I love her so much and appreciate our understanding and what she does to help people, I just couldn't cope with it."

Vicky was walking toward their car.

"Deal with it when the time comes," Parkman said.

"I only hope I can."

Chapter 13

MIKE DRAGGED THE HEAVY snake cage down the wide stairs until he reached the dolly. After strapping the cage to the dolly, he pushed it to the makeshift loading dock at the back of the building.

He backed a van up to the dock in near darkness as he didn't want to light the place up. It was after three in the morning with virtually no traffic out front, but still, risks weren't necessary.

Mike couldn't think of a time when he was happier, except when he slaughtered his parents on their vacation. That was a good day. He enjoyed branding their dead skin with upside-down crosses as the knife sliced through their throats and his parents' heads lopped off. Let the investigators run around looking for a crazed religious killer.

His parents had been rich. After their death, all their assets were liquidated, and the money was put into a trust fund. But now the fund was almost empty, the money running out. The fact that the church was a business, a rich business, wasn't lost on him. The ability to funnel money from the church undetected had been easy until recently. Several priests had set a meeting to discuss missing funds, and he wasn't invited.

It inspired him to murder those Catholic priests for all the hatred and death the Catholics had spread worldwide with their religious wars. Sure, Islam had their Jihad, and governments fought wars over oil, but the Catholics had killed more people worldwide than any other religion. Yet, it was the largest religion on Earth, followed by more people than any other.

"If you can't beat 'em, join 'em."

Mike left the van, left the driver's side door ajar, walked around to the back, and opened the doors. He carefully rolled the dolly to the edge of the loading dock and set the cage just inside the van. Once the cage was unstrapped, he pulled the dolly back. After a small push with his shoulder, he could shut and secure the back doors, the python safely inside.

He stepped back and admired the building they were supposed to turn into a non-profit site for the homeless.

Not anymore. Not after they find two dead bodies inside.

He ran around to the front of the van and grabbed the cross with Father George's name engraved in it. With his oxygen mask in hand, he headed back inside.

From the small viewing window, Father George hadn't moved. Mike donned the mask, ensured he got ample oxygen and unlocked the door. An audible whoosh accompanied the breaking of the seal.

Getting caught with one of his kills would stop him from

succeeding in his mission, and he didn't want to upset the Great One, so he rushed over to Father George and set the cross on his chest without nailing it in.

Mike backed into the hall, slammed the door, and stared at the ceiling. In the room above him, his beloved Evelyn lay dead.

"You weren't supposed to go yet," he mumbled inside the mask.

When he cleared the doorway, he tore off the mask and tossed it onto the floor. Then took a deep breath to repeat the words unfettered by the mask and instantly came down with a hacking cough. Some of the toxic gas must have filtered out further than he thought.

He leaned on the wall and coughed harder, trying to clear his lungs. On each intake, more gas entered him. Before it could overcome him, he started down the hall. Ultimately, he turned right and headed to the van, coughing as he went. It had abated some by the time he got to the back door.

Once outside, he stopped at the sight of three people walking by on the street.

He dropped and hid behind the van. They were too far away for him to hear what they were saying. He coughed under his breath, forcing his mouth to stay closed. After a moment, he crawled to the corner of the van and peeked around toward the street.

The three people had stopped. They stood quietly just outside the direct glow of a streetlight, their faces in the darkness.

Can they see me?

They probably heard the back door open and close, but he didn't think they could hear his coughing. Which meant they were waiting for someone to materialize. He couldn't wait them out. There was too much risk of being caught here.

Why would someone stand and watch the back of a loading dock?

Unless they were looking for something unusual. Something that didn't fit.

Unless they were cops.

There was no way he could tell from here. But if they were cops and tried to stop him, he would have to kill them. He had a gun in the glove box.

On his feet again, he coughed once more, then pulled the van keys out. He walked around the side of the van and hopped in.

"Excuse me," a female yelled.

He slammed his door. The trio started toward him.

He kept his head down as he turned the ignition. When he dropped it in gear, he looked up. Two of the three people were jogging his way. A man and a woman. The third person stayed back, standing at an odd angle.

He let his foot off the brake and pulled away from the loading dock.

As he turned the van toward the road, his headlights flashed on the pair. The man looked familiar, but he couldn't place him.

The woman was another story. He recognized her instantly. She was one of the bitches from the restaurant's parking lot where he had met Evelyn. He'd seen her a dozen times. She was the one who had followed them back here a few nights ago. He'd almost led her right to this building. It wouldn't have mattered because he had vacated for good tonight, but she had seen his face when he had picked up

Eve.

Eve was supposed to be with him right now. When they find Eve's body in the building, the police will interview her co-workers. This woman would know what he looked like.

He was getting close to the man and woman jogging toward him. Mike yanked on the wheel and jammed the accelerator to the floor as he was about to pass her.

The woman didn't have a chance.

Her head thunked on the van's hood, and then she fell under its tires. As the woman went under, blood hit the windshield.

Eve had talked about the woman after she had followed them that night. He couldn't remember her name. The van's front wheels bounced over her body, the suspension in the back bouncing a second time.

He swung the van toward the road and saw why the third person hadn't approached as fast as the other two.

She had a cast on her left foot and a crutch under one arm. It was the same girl from the crime scene last night.

The van had corrected too far toward the road to turn it back around and aim at her. Her death would have to wait.

"But mark my words," Mike said to himself. "I will come after you. I will learn your name and where you live, and then I will find you. Nothing will stop me from sending you to my master." He coughed. "Nothing will stop me from sending you to Hell."

He smiled as an idea came to him.

"That'll work. I'll wait for her tonight. She can die within hours."

He continued down the road, knowing he would see her again very soon.

Chapter 14

SARAH STOOD STILL FOR an extra second to catch her breath. She had her balance for the moment and was afraid to move lest she lose it.

A man had exited a door at the back of the darkened loading dock. He hesitated behind his vehicle too long, as if in hiding. Then he suddenly appeared, got in his van, and when Parkman and Vicky ran toward him, he swerved into Vicky, crushing her.

It all happened so fast. Vicky didn't have a chance. She barely had a chance to go for her weapon.

Sarah started forward, using her crutch like an expert as she hobbled to Vicky's side. Parkman was on his phone, screaming something into it about the location. He ran away to find a street sign.

As Sarah approached Vicky, she tossed the crutch aside and dropped to one knee. Blood seeped out each side of

Vicky's mouth. Her chest was caved in where the front of the van had connected with her body. She stared up at the stars, her eyes clouding over as her breath grew more labored and ragged.

"It'll be okay, Vicky," Sarah said. It was all she could think to say at the moment. "Just breathe. Force it in and out. Come on, Vicky, you can do it." She held Vicky's hand. "Parkman has help coming. Just hang in there."

Vicky looked toward Sarah. Their eyes locked for a moment as she took her last breath. Her chest lowered, then stilled. The life left her eyes.

Sarah took a deep breath, shuddered, then lowered Vicky's eyelids.

Parkman ran up. "Oh shit," he mumbled.

"Help me to my feet," Sarah said.

Parkman grabbed her under the arms and pulled her to one foot. She kept the broken one off the ground until he handed her the crutch.

"Police and ambulance are on their way," he said.

"They're not going to like this."

"Agreed. We're not even supposed to be here. This looks bad, Sarah. Especially with how the cops feel about you. Maybe you should let me handle this one." He handed the car keys to her. "Take the car. Come back in half an hour as if you're coming to pick me up. Go, before anyone gets here."

"Parkman, he was familiar."

"What?"

"The driver of the van was familiar. I've seen his face before."

"Where? Can you remember?"

"No, but when I do, we'll find him. We owe Hirst that

now."

Parkman looked down at Vicky's body. "We owe her that, too."

Sarah started away from him, knowing he was right. Another dead cop and Sarah was involved. There was no way the LAPD would believe she wasn't involved somehow.

She made it to their rental before the first siren wailed in the distance.

Once inside the car, she fired it up and sped away, leaving Parkman to stand alone over Vicky's dead body.

Her goal of helping the police and redeeming herself with Parkman quickly evaporated.

Unless things turned around, there wouldn't be enough sand in the world for Sarah to hide her head in.

Chapter 15

MIKE DROVE TWO CITY blocks and pulled into a coffee shop's parking lot. He turned around and pulled back out onto the road. After he went a block back the way he had come, he pulled over and waited in an area where the streetlights didn't reach him.

While waiting for the girl, he would have no choice but to leave if the area got too covered with emergency vehicles. The front grill of the van was dented and marked with blood. He needed to discard the vehicle, but not before he dealt with his python.

He would do if there were a way to kill the girl with the broken foot tonight.

He grabbed a crucifix from the box from behind the passenger seat. While he waited, he took his knife and began to cut a name into the wood. Since he didn't know her name, he carved "whore."

Up ahead, the same car from last night pulled onto Sunset Boulevard, going the other way. The driver was alone.

The girl with the broken foot.

He tossed the crucifix across the seat and, leaving his headlights off, got into position to follow.

The car turned a corner up ahead. When it was out of sight, he flicked the lights on, then turned the same corner. Three blocks up, the vehicle angled into a tiered parking garage attached to a large shopping mall.

He pulled over and waited.

What is she doing?

Half a minute later, her headlights flashed by as she hit the second level. Then again, on the third.

He realized she was driving to the top where she could wait, hidden from street view, and watch the action from up there. She would hit the top of the parkade in less than a minute and exit her vehicle. When she looked down, she would recognize his van.

Mike hit the gas as he saw her headlights flash on the last turn near the fifth level. His heart raced as he neared the entrance to the parking garage. Could he make it in time before she got out and looked down?

Without checking to see if she was looking, he turned into the entrance of the parking garage, which brought him under the protection of the levels above.

He let out the breath he had been holding. On the first level, there were only two vehicles at this hour. The garage had a soft orange glow from the night lights.

Mike retrieved the gun from the glove box and checked to see if it was loaded.

He released the brake and started toward the ramp.

There was irony in ascending toward Heaven to kill the meddling woman and send her to Hell.

Chapter 16

SARAH REACHED THE TOP of the parking garage, pulled forward into a spot with the lowest retaining wall so she could look over it, got out, and left the car door open.

She looked down over the mid-thigh high ledge. The shopping mall's parking garage was too far away to see the building where Vicky had been hit.

She would wait half an hour and then drive over to pick up Parkman. There would be questions, too many, and the answers would have to be made up, but they'd get through it. They always did. She had faith in Parkman's plan.

Nothing moved on the street below. It was nearing four in the morning. In a few hours, the mall would crawl with cars. But she'd be long gone by then.

She got back in the rental, rolled the window down, and turned the car off. A half-hour wasn't too long, but it was long enough for a power nap.

The soft breeze coming through the window calmed her. A lot had happened in a short while. When she was done in Canada, she had made plans to meet Aaron in Santa Rosa, where she was headed to recuperate and let her foot heal. The chance to help Parkman came up, and she took it. But not before Aaron, in Toronto, had already bought his plane ticket for California.

Hopefully, the craziness in L.A. would be over soon so she could get home and have some much-needed rest and quality time with Aaron. Until then, he would have to hang around with her parents.

She closed her eyes and rested her head on the back of the seat. A siren in the distance beat rhythmically.

"Ten minutes," she whispered. "Maybe fifteen."

She drifted off with thoughts of Aaron on her mind and how crazy their relationship was. The only things keeping them apart were murderers, rapists, and cannibals.

Not your average relationship.

Her lips twitched, attempting a smile as she fell into a light sleep.

Chapter 17

PARKMAN HAD TOLD TWO different investigators what had happened, but now they wanted him to tell another man who would arrive at any minute.

Officers entered the back of the building with probable cause. What would make the van driver try to run people over in his attempt to escape?

Another detective was on the phone trying to ascertain who owned the building as Vicky's body was loaded into the ambulance that would take her to her last stop before embalming.

Parkman watched all this in a detached manner. He had been to countless crime scenes in his life and even caused a few himself.

The hardest ones were when a cop was involved or killed. The look on the faces of every officer here was a mix of sadness and anger.

Detective David Hirst was called in. The only reason Parkman was here was that Detective Hirst had requested his help with the priest killings, but they were way off track with that now.

All Parkman had was the description of a white van with a dented grill. It had been too dark, and Parkman was too busy jumping out of the way of the van to get the license plate.

An unmarked cruiser pulled up. The lights turned off, and the door opened.

Detective Hirst.

"Shit, here we go," Parkman whispered.

Hirst spotted Parkman and started toward him.

A man came running out of the back door of the building, coughing, and hacking. Another man followed the first, also coughing. Both men dropped to their knees, gasping for air.

Parkman ran across the gravel lot to see what was going on. Hirst called out from behind him, but he kept going.

Other officers raced over to help their fallen colleagues. One of the men on his knees got helped up. He coughed a couple of more times, then tried to speak.

"Dead … another priest."

What?

"Some kind of toxic gas …" the officer coughed. So hard this time, Parkman expected blood, but none came. "A cross." The cop pointed at his throat. "Just like the other murders."

Someone grabbed Parkman's arm and tried to spin him around.

"What are you doing here?" Hirst asked. "Come on, Parkman. This is a crime scene, and you're supposed to be out of Los Angeles already."

As Parkman let Hirst drag him away, the officer stopped coughing long enough to say, "There's a girl upstairs. She's dead, too. It doesn't"—he coughed into his hands—"look good."

Parkman tore his arm out of Hirst's grasp and stepped closer to the crowd of cops.

"The girl's name is probably Evelyn Wynn," Parkman said loud enough for everyone to hear. "The priest killer called her Eve. Her street name was Mercedes. Vicky Chard was run over because Vicky knew what the priest killer looked like." Parkman wiped his mouth and stepped closer to Hirst. "Find the white van; you find the priest killer."

Chapter 18

As he turned onto the ramp that led to the fifth level of the parking garage, Mike flicked off the headlights. He placed the gun in his lap and maneuvered around the curved ramp, easing to the top slowly so as not to alert the girl. The night sky came into view as the van leveled out, but the woman's car was nowhere to be seen. It took him a second to realize he had gotten turned around as he ascended. The van now faced the shopping mall and not the road.

He turned the vehicle around and started for the other side of the large parking floor. As he cleared a stairwell enclosure, the car came into view. Parked forward in a spot aimed at the road, it was the only vehicle on the fifth level. The parking garage was higher than any other building within three city blocks. No witnesses would be able to see this high up.

He stopped the van five feet behind her car. He slipped

the gun into his left hand and eased the safety off. It would be terribly disappointing to just shoot her. What he had come up with was genius, and he looked forward to it.

With his left hand out the van's window, ready to fire if she tried to run, he eased up to four feet behind her Chevy Cruz, blocking her ability to back out. He cut the engine and waited. He could see her head. She didn't move. He had to be careful and play this right, or it wouldn't work. She might have seen him when he approached and called the police, and now she was just waiting to be rescued. She might have a gun and waited for him to exit the vehicle. Or she could simply be asleep, although he doubted that. Luck wasn't that kind to him.

Maybe he should just ram her vehicle from behind. He could push her car through the small concrete railing and over the ledge with enough force. Had to be at least a fifty-foot drop to the street below.

It was a woman who the snake tempted in the Garden of Eden, and it would be a woman who would die by the snake here.

He grabbed the roll of silver duct tape that had worked so well on Eve's mouth and quietly opened the van's door. Mike slipped out of the vehicle, the gun in one hand, the tape in the other. Before he went too far, he adjusted his ball cap lower on his head to cover his face.

It wasn't her he was worried about. The girl wouldn't leave this parking garage alive. But there were hidden cameras everywhere. This parking garage may have a few recording him right now. The van wouldn't matter. He would leave the snake with the girl and had no further use of the van. The police would find it aflame before sunrise and all evidence linked to him smoldering.

With the gun ready, he stepped closer, his finger inside the trigger guard. He lowered the gun when he stood beside her open window, his lips parting in a wide smile.

Luck was being kind, after all. She was asleep. What a gift. It couldn't have been better.

He tossed the duct tape inside her car. It bounced off the center console and came to rest on the passenger seat. The girl stirred in her sleep but didn't fully wake.

He looked closely at her face and confirmed it was the same girl from last night's crime scene.

The best way to wake her up was to shoot her in a non-fatal manner. The only issue was the noise. But with no one around at this hour, it didn't matter much.

He switched the gun to his right hand, eased it inside the open window, and aimed at the foot with the cast.

Her face was serene, peaceful. She was probably getting some much needed sleep.

"Sorry about this," he whispered. "It's just not your day."

He took careful aim and fired. A hole formed in the side of her black medical boot as she jerked awake.

What was louder than the gun going off was the woman's startled scream in his ear before he could pull the gun back out of the window.

To silence her, he backhanded her in the mouth.

Her head rocked back, smacked the headrest, and righted again.

Before she could turn the car on or try to get out, he pointed the gun at her face and said loud enough to be heard over her voice, "Stay right where you are. Don't move."

She writhed in the front seat, but to her credit, she didn't shout again. Her eyes were wide and bloodshot from being woken up in such a brutal fashion. She stared at him insanely, probably trying to figure out what was happening.

"Grab the duct tape beside you," he ordered.

She continued to stare with those intense eyes without moving for the tape.

"Grab the duct tape, or I'll shoot you through the teeth." He paused, then said, "Do it now."

Chapter 19

PARKMAN EXPLAINED TO HIRST how he knew Evelyn's name and why he was there with Officer Chard. They were about to enter the building to view the bodies when a report echoed in the distance.

"Did you hear that?" Parkman asked.

"What?"

"I thought I just heard a gun." He raised his hand and pointed. "From that way."

"Seriously?"

Parkman met Hirst's eyes. "Yes. Seriously. And Sarah's not far. She's out there somewhere. She took the car to follow the white van."

"Okay. We've got a dozen officers too many on this scene. I'll ask a couple units to cruise the area."

"Thanks," Parkman said as he stepped through the door.

Hirst didn't follow him right away. Parkman heard him

tell some men to get in their cars and search the area. It impressed Parkman that Hirst could describe the rental without having to ask. He must've remembered it from the night before when they attended the body on Mulholland Drive.

Once inside, Parkman wished he had a toothpick. The crime scene was being dealt with carefully because of the toxic gas. No one was touching that room until they isolated what kind of gas it was and how to neutralize it.

But the girl's body on the floor above was being processed. Parkman watched the crime scene experts do their thing as he grew more upset at how close they had come to stopping the priest killer.

Hirst joined him. "Come on outside, Parkman. There's nothing we can do for her now."

Parkman followed Hirst and, for the first time, wondered about Sarah and her safety. Should she be here in Los Angeles with a broken ankle? But negotiating her early exit from L.A. would be impossible. She would stay on until the perp was caught. It was his fault in the first place. What made him think he could ask Sarah to come to southern California within days of almost being killed by a sadistic cannibal in Canada?

He couldn't blame Hirst. Doing him a favor should have involved only Parkman, but Hirst had asked for Sarah. Parkman selfishly thought he'd get a chance to work with Sarah and be close to her in L.A. Maybe they could bond again, as the incident behind her parents' home in Santa Rosa still bothered her. He needed her to see his side. He needed her to know that he forgave her and would probably do what she had done if the tables had been turned.

The distant sky had lightened with the first sign of sunrise and another gorgeous day.

Parkman walked past Hirst and headed for the road.

"Where're you going?"

"Be right back."

At the road, he looked toward Sunset Boulevard, the way Sarah had gone with the car. Why wasn't she back yet?

Hirst stepped up beside him. "You okay?" When Parkman didn't respond, he said, "Waiting for someone?"

"Sarah said she would be here by now." He met Hirst's eyes. "Just getting worried for her."

"I heard what happened in Bing's parking lot. Sorry about how my fellow officers treated her."

Parkman wiped his face, exhaustion and frustration setting in.

Sarah, where are you?

Hirst put a hand on his back. "Come on, Parkman. There's nothing we can do standing around. Let's examine some of the evidence. Maybe we'll see something new. It'll be good to keep busy until Sarah returns to pick you up."

Parkman knew that keeping busy wouldn't keep his mind off Sarah. It would only make him antsier while he waited.

Chapter 20

WHAT HAD SHE DONE? How could she have fallen into such a deep sleep so fast to have not heard the van approach?

Then she remembered the weapons Parkman had managed to get. The hammer lay under the car seat on her side. If only she could get to it.

"The duct tape," the man repeated.

Keeping her eyes on him, she felt around the passenger seat until her fingers found the roll. She picked it up.

"Good," he whispered. "Use your right hand to secure your left to the steering wheel. Do it now."

Slowly, with the barrel of his gun two inches from her cheek, Sarah rolled out a foot of tape and grabbed the top of the wheel with her left hand. Then she applied the tape and looped it around twice before cutting it with her teeth.

"Now, hand me the duct tape."

As he took it, she dropped away from him and lunged

across the console for the base of the passenger seat. The steering wheel turned as her secured left hand yanked it toward her, but since the car was off, the wheel resisted. Fully extended, her right hand stopped one inch from the hammer's handle. She pushed harder as he grabbed for her hair. It was hopeless. The hammer was out of reach. Her eyes watered at the sharp pain of having her hair yanked. She groaned as she was forced back up to a sitting position.

"What are you doing?" he asked. "I have a gun. Are you a simpleton?"

He released her hair, grabbed her right hand, and jammed it onto the steering wheel. He set the gun on the car's roof, yanked a strip of tape out, and leaned in to wrap it around her right wrist, locking her hands in the ten and two o'clock positions on the wheel.

Sarah lunged forward when he was in front of her, mouth open. When her teeth clamped down, the man's left ear lobe was caught between them.

He screamed as he tried to yank his head out of the car, but Sarah held on tight, her teeth gnashing back and forth to sever his flesh and take her pound.

His elbow smashed into the center of her chest once. Then again.

Out of the corner of her eye, she saw him reach for the gun on the roof. She thought about getting shot again for a brief moment, but then she was probably dead anyway if she let him go.

Suddenly his ear was clear of her teeth, and he retreated. The thin part of the lobe was all she had gotten. The copper taste of blood filled her mouth. She spit out the offending chunk of skin, blood splattering on the steering wheel and dash.

The man held a hand over his bleeding ear as he stumbled away.

She watched him in her mirrors. She applied her teeth to the top of the duct tape when he was at the van and bit down.

Moments later, the cold tip of the gun jammed against her head.

"Sit back," he said.

She stopped biting, having only made a small teeth mark in the thick tape. Slowly, she leaned back in the car seat and turned to face him.

His ear still dripped blood, the bite deep enough that it wouldn't clot too fast. He held a small cage filled with mice, two of them quite fat.

"What's this? You're going to rodent me to death? Never saw that one coming." She smiled, knowing blood still covered her teeth.

He opened the cage door and tilted it so all the mice would fall onto Sarah's lap. Each one landed in and around her legs. A couple of them scurried up and down the length of her one thigh, others jumped and hit the floor, preferring to hide under her car seat.

"Here's my friend's dinner," the man said. "He won't need this anymore."

"Mice don't scare me." She looked up at him, more than half his face covered by the bill of the hat. "I'm not your average girl. Tell me you've got something worse."

"Your wish is my command."

He disappeared from the window. She lunged forward, her teeth going to work on the tape. With no need to check on him, she bit and bit until a portion of the tape surrendered to her teeth.

He reappeared beside her as she pulled back on the flap she had cut out of the tape. She ignored him, knowing she had to get her hands free. Or at least one of them.

Something heavy touched her lap. There was no point in taking her teeth off the job to see what it was. She was almost free. Freedom meant she could fight. She could get to the hammer. She could turn the car on and ram his vehicle.

He set something behind her. It felt like a thick pillow, like the circular kind someone would use for lumbar support or for under their knees when resting on a massage table.

Then the tape snapped off her right wrist. Her hand was free. She grabbed the car keys that sat idle in the ignition and twisted them, turning the car on. But something blocked her arm from the center console where she had wanted to drop the car into reverse to ram his van.

Something squeezed her belly. She looked down. Repulsed, she reared up and tried to push the snake off, but it didn't budge. She took a deep breath, held it, and began hammering at the snake's body with her one free hand as it wrapped another loop around her.

"My gift to you," the man said. "That's an African Rock Python. He hasn't eaten in a month. Quite hungry, actually." He stood back and watched as the snake wrapped itself around her again, locking her upper arms against her body. "He smells the scent of the rodents on you, so naturally, he thinks you're food. Since he can eat deer, pigs, and dogs, you'll do just fine."

Only able to move her right arm below the elbow and unsure if the snake was venomous, Sarah could only watch as it slithered around her again, tightening as it went. The thickness of its body was impressive and intimidating at the same time, and its strength was intense.

The snake wanted to crush her as it started to squeeze. She held her breath, waiting to see what would happen next, her mind racing on possible options.

"You see where the snake has bit into the back of your car seat." He leaned in closer. "Oh wait, I guess you're all tied up. You can't turn around and see. Well, anyway, you got lucky because this kind of python usually bites the victim to lock onto its prey and then begins the death wrap."

"Death wrap?" she managed to say, a tiny amount of breath coming out with the words.

When she spoke, the snake tightened again.

Shit! Won't do that again.

"Feel fortunate that she didn't bite you. My precious snake has many sharp teeth that are curved backward. Pythons have attacked and killed humans before, so you won't be the only one."

Breathing became a chore. Sarah struggled under its power but was not even able to lean forward as its teeth clung to the shoulder of the car seat, its body locked on her, keeping her back.

Absolutely helpless, her lungs yearning for air, her mind raced. There was no way to get to the hammer on the passenger seat floor. Whatever would stop this snake and allow Sarah to live had to come to her within half a minute, or she'd have to expel her breath. Letting it out meant the snake would tighten more, refusing to allow her the life-giving breath she needed.

"A snake tempted Eve," the man rambled on beside her. "And now a snake takes you to Hell. Goodbye, whore.

You're no better than Lot's wife. If I could, I would've turned you into a pillar of salt."

The man headed back toward his van.

Sarah struggled, the mirror reflecting her red face and blood on her lips.

The man watched her from inside his vehicle. The rental car was still running, but her arms were locked up. She couldn't reach the center console.

In desperation, she let out a tiny amount of air and tried to suck in as much air as she could, but at the exact second her ribcage constricted, the snake tightened, cutting off any chance to catch even the tiniest amount of air.

She would be dead in under a minute, crushed under the power of the snake, unless she thought of something.

The van's headlights came on behind her. He started backing up.

A horrible idea came upon her. A last resort.

Her rental was still idling. She brought her right knee up to the gear shift, pressed the black button, and pushed the shift back one spot into reverse.

It worked just as her lungs screamed for release.

As the car reversed, she hit the gas and pressed back against the seat. The car raced backward until it smashed into the van's grill.

Breath escaped her lungs again. The snake tightened. She wanted to scream with the pain as her ribs were about to break.

She pushed the gear shift into neutral with her knee, then drive.

The man jumped out of his van and ran at her, the gun aimed.

She hit the gas, her lungs about to release the air whether she wanted to or not. If she exhaled, her rib cage would collapse under the snake's intense pressure.

She slammed the accelerator to the floor on her last surge of strength, her last chance at life. The car jerked forward, away from the madman with the gun running after her, toward the short concrete abutment at the edge of the parking garage on the fifth floor.

There was hope if it was possible to hit the abutment and whack the snake with the airbags. If not, she was out of options.

The edge came fast.

The gun fired behind her. The back window shattered. Another shot embedded in the dash by the stereo, missing her by inches.

Maybe he'll hit the snake and kill it.

Suddenly, through the windshield, the abutment looked too small.

Her lungs didn't just wail for air; they threatened to collapse on their own as the car hit the concrete, jerking it to an almost complete stop, the back end lifting, then dropping down hard with the violence of the impact.

The airbags didn't deploy, but most of the abutment broke off and fell more than fifty feet to the street below. The car dangled on the edge, more on solid ground than air.

She opened her mouth to breathe, knowing it was her last decision and that the snake was waiting for that moment.

Another bullet slammed into the dash, closer this time.

She let out some air as she hit the gas. The back tires caught on something and pushed the rental car forward.

She released the rest of the pent-up air in her lungs and

tried to breathe as the car teetered over the edge of the parking garage, but no air came.

At the same moment, the car slipped over the edge and began a free fall for the concrete below, Sarah pushed against the snake with her arms to get air into her lungs as the snake tightened even more.

For a brief moment, there was silence. Then the wind increased as the ground raced toward the windshield.

See you soon, Vivian.

A tear rolled out of her right eye.

"Fuck you, snake," Sarah whispered the second before the grill was decimated by the impact that continued into the engine, jamming everything toward the passenger compartment.

One moment she was in a quiet free fall, the next crashing into the concrete five stories below, face first.

Her last wish was that the airbags weren't defective.

Chapter 21

More gunfire in the distance. It had to be Sarah.

"Take me that way." Parkman pointed to where he heard the sound.

"Come on," Hirst said.

They ran for the detective's cruiser. Hirst squealed out of the area, a red flashing light on his roof.

When they were two blocks away, Hirst's radio sounded. Gunfire had been heard, and there was a car accident within four blocks of Vicky's murder scene.

"What the hell is going on tonight?" Parkman asked.

"We don't know if they're related."

"True. But it's likely."

After two more turns, Hirst swung onto the road that led to a mall. Parkman saw the flashing lights of a police cruiser parked on either side of a ruined car that sat more on the edge of the sidewalk than the road. From a distance, Parkman couldn't tell what the vehicle had hit that would cause that kind of damage.

When Hirst stopped the cruiser, Parkman got out. At first, he didn't recognize the damaged vehicle, but as he walked closer, he could tell it was the same color as their rental.

A sickening feeling filled his gut. For a brief second, his step faltered. It all came together in the next moment. He looked up and saw that the edge of the concrete railing on the fifth floor was broken. The car must have been pushed off. The trunk had damage that wasn't consistent with hitting the ground.

But all that could be figured out later.

He ran to the driver's side. One of the officers waved him off, but Hirst motioned, and the officer stepped back.

Parkman dropped to his knees as sirens wailed behind him.

Sarah was scrunched up in an impossible position. Blood covered her face and ran down her neck. Her head and chest rested against the airbag like a pillow. He touched her neck and felt for a pulse.

He couldn't feel one.

He tried again.

A faint pulse at the base of her jaw beat under the touch of his finger.

"She's alive!" he shouted for Hirst.

Vehicles stopped behind him.

"Sarah's alive!" he shouted again.

What looked like a snake was wrapped in layers around her chest and parts of the seat.

"What the hell happened here?" someone said.

A hand landed on his shoulder.

"Hey man, paramedics are here, and we also have firemen here. Please step back so we can extricate the young woman."

Stunned, Parkman stood up and allowed himself to be led away from the ruined rental car.

Nobody hurt Sarah and got away with it.

Nobody.

Chapter 22

FATHER ADAMS WAS SHOCKED at what had happened in one of the buildings the church had bought. He was disgusted that the man responsible had stolen a church vehicle, run down a police officer, and tried to kill the guest, Sarah Roberts, whom the police had asked to come help with the investigation.

He entered the hospital through the main sliding doors and started for the admissions desk.

"Good morning." Father Adams spoke in his usual deep cadence when he wore the suit with his white collar. "I'm looking for a woman admitted recently. Her name is Sarah Roberts."

The nurse shuffled papers aside, found her computer mouse, and clicked.

"Can I have the name again?" she asked.

"Sarah Roberts," Father Adams said, his voice patient.

"I'm sorry, Father, are you family? Otherwise ..." The nurse looked up. Adams could tell she wanted to help him as most people wanted to help a man of God, but something on her computer had cautioned her.

"Check the list of approved names," he said. "You'll see that Father Adams is on it."

The woman clicked her mouse, then smiled before looking up. "You're right. They're expecting you. She's on the second floor. Room 206."

"Thank you."

Father Adams walked away from the counter, passed the elevators, and headed for the sign that showed the stairs. Once on the stairs, he pulled out his rosary and adjusted his jacket.

On the second floor, he opened the door to chaos. Two nurses ran by pushing a stretcher. Another nurse called out a doctor's name. Two people, one a patient having issues walking while the other held him up, leaned against the wall by the stairwell door, evidently making little progress to wherever they were headed.

Two young kids ran down the hall so fast they missed the nurse's warning to walk.

Father Adams took it all in for a moment, breathed deep, then read the sign on the door across the hallway. He was four doors away from Sarah's room. He started down the hall, nodded slightly to the couple leaning on the wall, stepped aside to let another stretcher pass, and made it to the police officer sitting in a chair outside room 206.

"Must be a long shift," Father Adams said when he saw the three empty coffee cups at the officer's feet.

"Yes, Father," the officer said as he looked at a list on his clipboard. "Father Adams?"

"In the flesh."

"Go right in. They're waiting for you."

Father Adams pushed on the door and entered the room. Detective Hirst stood by the window. A man sat in a chair on the side, and Sarah lay in the bed, her eyes closed, a couple of bandages on her face, and the bed covers up to her chin.

"Gentlemen," he said softly, letting the door close behind him.

Hirst turned around, and the man in the chair got up and approached. They shook hands.

"Glad you could come. I'm Parkman."

"I saw you the night Father Alvin was found. You're Sarah's friend?"

He nodded. "We came to Los Angeles together to help Detective Hirst with his case."

Father Adams turned to Hirst. "And how is that going, Detective?"

"I'm sorry about Father George," Hirst said. "When you're done here, we need to go through all the people who would have access to your vehicles and buildings." Hirst coughed into his hand, wiped his mouth, and continued. "The case has shifted. We are now looking for a local man who we suspect works for the church."

Father Adams stepped deeper into the room. He moved toward the bed and looked down at Sarah's sleeping form.

"Will she be okay?" he asked.

Hirst nodded. Parkman moved around Adams and stood by the head of the bed, almost like he was protecting her.

"She'll pull through," Parkman said.

"How badly was she hurt?" Adams asked.

"One cracked rib, a lot of bruising, and a few cuts on her face, but otherwise, she's fine. She was shot in her broken foot, but the Robo boot deflected the bullet. No harm at all."

"Tough lady." Father Adams turned his attention toward the detective again. "Tell me, how is it you suspect a member of the church? Couldn't it be someone who stole our vehicle and broke into that building?"

Detective Hirst stepped closer to Adams, almost confrontational. "Father George was lured to that building. He walked into that sealed room where the gas killed him. At no time was he secured in any way. No markings on his wrists. He wouldn't walk into that building, and that room, under his own steam unless he knew the man that accompanied him. Whoever is doing this works for the Catholic church or is a part of it in some capacity."

Father Adams looked at Sarah. "Sounds reasonable." He clasped his hands in front of him. "There are a lot of people who work with the church and for the church. Deciding which person you're looking for could become a challenge."

Both men held a defiant posture as if Father Adams was the threat. He attributed their gruffness to having to deal with what happened to Sarah.

"We aren't too worried about locating this man," Parkman said.

"How's that?" Adams asked.

"Sarah here. She's alive. The perp tried to use a snake to kill her. When the firemen pulled her out of the vehicle, and the paramedics got to her, we were all amazed that she was in one piece. The snake died from the fall when its head smacked the dash and was severed by a piece of glass. It was wrapped around Sarah, which provided another layer of cushioning for her. What tried to kill her only saved her, and when she wakes, she will tell us who the man was. She has seen his face, we're sure."

"Praise the Lord," Father Adams said. "Gentlemen, I look forward to the end of this horrific siege." He turned to Detective Hirst. "Please, come by any time, and I will open my doors to the investigation at the church level. You can have access to all our staff."

"I appreciate that, Father."

"Until then, gentlemen, I wish her a speedy recovery and bid you both farewell."

Father Adams pivoted and started for the door.

"Father?"

He stopped, his hand on the doorknob.

"Yes, Detective?"

"You were the last to meet with Father George before he left the church yesterday, weren't you?"

Adams turned back around to face Hirst. "As a matter of fact, I was. How would you come by this information?"

"When asking about Father George at the church, people said they saw you two talking. Can you tell me what you discussed and where he might have been heading afterward?"

"Our discussion was of a private matter, a church matter, but I can assure you it had nothing to do with his death or this issue."

"Were you aware of Father George's history before he came to Los Angeles? What he was suspected of?"

"Am I being interrogated?" Father Adams asked.

Detective Hirst exchanged a glance with Parkman. Then he turned back to Adams.

"Can we meet in your office in a couple of hours? Say

around two in the afternoon?"

"Absolutely. I'll be there all day."

"Fair enough. And Father, what happened to your ear?"

"Oh, this." Father Adams touched the bandage at the base of his lobe. "I took a shortcut through the trees behind my church, where I slipped and fell. A branch caught my ear and sliced part of the bottom off. Not a big thing, actually." He opened the door. "Gentlemen."

He pulled the door closed behind him, nodded at the cop in the chair, and headed out of the hospital, his step a little quicker.

Chapter 23

Sarah sat up in her hospital bed and pulled the food tray closer. Awake for an hour, Parkman was filling her in on everything the authorities were doing to locate the man who killed Vicky.

"I still don't know how my injuries are so minimal after falling from the fifth floor in that car," Sarah said. "Grateful but mystified."

Hospital food was getting better. A quinoa salad with a green juice to wash it all down.

"There was no weight in the back of the car," Parkman offered. "Once the engine planted itself in the concrete, and the airbags did their job, it's as if you had a head-on collision. Maybe Vivian made your body go limp somehow to protect you."

Sarah shook her head between bites. "Amazing." She wiped her mouth, then pushed the half-eaten salad away.

"What's wrong?" Parkman asked.

"Nothing, just thinking about what happened." She cocked her head sideways. "Something's coming."

"What do you mean?"

"Not sure. But I can feel it."

"That's interesting." Parkman leaned forward. "How do you feel it?"

"I was afraid you'd ask that." She looked at the window. "How high up are we?"

"Second floor."

"What's below that window?"

Parkman went to the window and opened it. He stuck his head out, looked around, and leaned back in. "We're facing the back of the hospital. There's a couple of ambulances parked right below us. What does that matter?"

Her eyes glazed over as the premonition washed through her. Vivian's presence was getting easier to feel, easier to channel.

"When the time comes, someone is going through that window. I just wanted to know what would catch the fall."

"Is it Vivian?" Parkman asked as he retook his seat.

Sarah nodded slowly.

"Tell me," Parkman said as he rubbed his hands together. "As an automatic writer, I've never asked you your stance on religion. You're in Los Angeles to help to stop the murders of Catholic priests, and I'm not even sure of your religion, your belief system."

Sarah slipped her fork under her right buttock, ensuring it was hidden.

"On one condition," she said.

"What's that?" Parkman asked.

"That you move when I say move. Do not hesitate. And do not try to save me. Deal?"

"What are you talking about?" Parkman started to stand.

Sarah raised a hand for him to sit. "There's no danger right this minute, but it's coming. Just move when I say so."

"Sarah, we have a cop stationed outside the door."

"Parkman, you're not listening. Whoever is coming will get past the cop. Everyone knows him. That's why he went after Vicky. She had seen his face. When he attacked me, he had a hat on. Just trust me. Move when I say so."

Parkman sat back, crossed his legs, and clasped his hands around his knee. "I'm ready when you are. I'll ask how high when you say jump. Until then, I want to hear your take on religion."

Sarah leaned back, rested her head on the pillow, and sighed deeply, closing her eyes.

"I have no issue with religion itself. In fact, I think religion is a good thing. It has helped so many people for centuries. It's the same for me with the police. They've helped so many people for centuries, and I love the fact that they're there. I just hate when policing goes bad, as with religion. I have zero use for a Holy War. Killing someone because of their beliefs is ridiculous and insane, but that won't stop anytime soon." She opened her eyes and stared at the ceiling. "Isn't a belief simply an opinion you're unwilling to reconsider? One person believes this, the other that. Ultimately they are only opinions, albeit strong ones."

"But what about *your* beliefs? Your personal idea of God?"

"I have a unique perspective."

"How so?"

"Vivian's essence has been working through me since I was eighteen. That's almost eight years now. I've developed a feeling of how most of it works. So my beliefs aren't just beliefs anymore; they're more fact-based. I don't have an opinion on the matter, just an understanding."

"Wow." Parkman sat back. "What could you possibly know? And with that knowledge, could you save us all? Start a new religion? Bring light to darkness?"

"Scared you might learn something you didn't expect? Something that'll shatter what you believe, your preconceived notion of God and religion? Make you reconsider your opinions on the matter?"

The hospital intercom in the hallway chimed. Parkman jumped at the sudden noise. A doctor was paged to attend to an emergency somewhere in the hospital.

"It's fine, Parkman. I'll give you ample notice before anything happens."

He nodded and uncrossed his legs.

"Before we come here to live our lives," Sarah started, "we write out our own life book with all the characters, our family and friends, and all the events of our lives all set in place. This extremely detailed book is the story of the life we're about to live here on Earth. But here's the neat part. You pick your parents, and they pick you. You choose your friends and your kids, if you have any, and everything else you want to experience while down here. Even the heartache. You pick everything in such detail that you and I rewrote even this conversation before hitting the womb all those years ago."

"Wow, that's wild. What's it all for? Why do we do it?"

"Have you ever lost something that eventually came

back? Like a pet that wandered away. For argument's sake, your cat was lost for a week; then suddenly, the cat comes back. How do you feel? Don't you hug that cat, give them special food and treat them like royalty after missing them for a week and knowing it might never return? Don't you appreciate that cat so much more than if it hadn't wandered away in the first place? Would you be smothering it in kisses, treating it like royalty, had the cat been there all week? That's what Heaven is."

"Tell me more."

"On the other side, we live in Heaven all the time. Because it's so amazing, we fail to realize how seriously amazing it is. It's almost like we become ungrateful. Like living with the cat, day in, day out. So we come down here, live our life book, and go home. Our return home is like when the cat came back. We appreciate it so much more. We can't believe how amazing it is after leaving this tough place."

"Then why is Earth so hard? Why not make it a little easier?"

She narrowed her eyes. "Some of this you're going to have to put together on your own, but I'll tell you what I've learned through Vivian." She adjusted herself. "The harder it is down here, the more you'll appreciate going home. And since God—the Supreme Being, the Enlightened One, the Prime Mover, even Yahweh, whatever people call him— made everything, it's all a part of him. We're a part of him. An actual part of the divinity. So one of the things we strive to do is evolve our soul for Him by coming here. We try to better ourselves, which is why we come down here in the first place. The real death is coming here. We're *born again* when we go home."

Parkman got up and started to pace. "Based on that, how does Satan fit into your beliefs? Where's the devil in the details?"

"There isn't one. There's no Satan. He's a fable written by man. There's no Hell, either. This is a fact, not a belief or an opinion. Earth is the closest thing to Hell. What we do to each other is hell enough. Someone once said, 'Religion is for people afraid of going to Hell. Spirituality is for people who have been there.'"

Parkman stopped pacing. "That's good. I like that. But some would argue that if there's a God, there has to be a devil."

"They can argue all they want. There's no devil." She used air quotes on the word *devil*. "God's counter are humans and the horrific things we do to each other, not Lucifer. Man wrote the Bible. I wouldn't tell too many people this, as I could be stoned for blasphemy, but I've learned this through Vivian. This is one of the reasons Vivian works through me. To ease some of the pain here on Earth." She took a drink of her green juice. "You remember Russell, my cousin?"

Parkman nodded as he stopped by the window to look out.

"Russell was an automatic writer, too. There are others out there doing good. He saved my life that day on the roof of that hotel in downtown Toronto."

"What's baffling me then is why do it in the first place?"

"What's it all for? The age-old question." Sarah finished her juice and set the cup on the tray with her unfinished salad. "It's all to experience His knowledge. Imagine the best marine biologist in the world who knew everything there ever was to know about marine biology. The guy knew it like you would know your phone number. He was a walking encyclopedia. But he'd never been to the ocean, seen plankton or shrimp, or taken in the salty air of the sea. That's how I understand God. He is all-knowing and experiences his knowledge through us and our experiences. Through all our five senses, all of us, all at once. We are living, breathing versions of his knowledge."

"Wow, a bit hard to grasp." Parkman stared out the window. "Doesn't he ever get disappointed?"

"Of course," Sarah said. "But never angry. Imagine a God of love giving his children an ultimatum. He would say, 'I'll give you no tangible proof of my existence, but you have to believe in me, or you'll burn in a lake of fire.'" Sarah laughed, then winced at the pain in her ribs. "Hilarious. All man-made fables. How would you feel if your child hurt someone, spent time in jail, and then knocked on your door at forty years of age? Would you hear his story? Would you at least let him in? So what does God think when his children—us—screw up and when it's all over, come home, our heads down? Especially when his capacity to love is a million times greater than us humans."

She looked at her cup, but the juice was gone. "That's Judgment Day. When you judge yourself in the end. When you die, your soul goes through a life review. I know this because Vivian had to go through it. During this life review, a white light asks, 'What have you done with the life I've given you?' or something like that. As your life flashes before your eyes, what hits you, in the presence of such peace and love are all the bad things you did and all the times you hurt someone. What you feel is the pain and suffering you caused others. You'll cry and judge yourself harshly. While this happens, you're in the presence of an all-forgiving, all-loving, all-caring entity who does this to help cleanse your soul of your earthly chattels and prepare you for entering your rightful place, your home."

Parkman took his seat again. "I have so many more questions. Can we continue?"

"Sure, but be ready. Something's coming soon. Or someone."

"Define soon."

"Any minute now." Sarah tightened her grip on the fork beside her.

"Should I be standing or sitting?"

"Won't matter."

He tented his fingers in front of him. "The suspense is killing me."

"Me too. You think I like this? I can feel it, like déjà vu. He's coming."

"There's something. What's your definition of déjà vu?"

"When we come here, our blueprint, the book we wrote for our life, is inside our subconscious. We take it everywhere we go like a guide, but we can't consciously read it. When we're on our right path, a small drip, a glimpse of our life book, falls into our conscious mind, and we feel like we've been in that spot before, even if we haven't. You can even tell the future at that moment, like if someone knocks on the door or the phone rings. That's déjà vu. When you're not on your life path, you don't experience it. If you stray too far, you end up with migraines, but I don't know much about that as most people are bound to follow their path."

"How does that work regarding free will? Why are there

so many religions, then? What about reincarnation? Is it possible?" He got out of his seat again. "Sarah, I've got a thousand questions."

"Vivian isn't here right now. At least I can't feel her. Most of what I told you is what I know from feeling her essence and sharing my body with her spirit for so long. But I do know one thing. Whether people believe in God or not, it doesn't matter because he believes in us. All of us go home. Even the murdering psychopaths we kill. All we're doing is getting them off this plane so the rest of us can enjoy life as best we can without their kind mucking things up for us. They go through their life review and purge a lot for all the shit they did down here."

"What about ghosts? Are they real?"

"Absolutely. They're earthbound spirits. People who have died under extreme conditions are bound to this plane by intense anger or love. Earthbound entities don't know they're dead and—"

A knock on the door silenced her.

"Go," Sarah said. Her hand came out and pointed at the window, the fork between her fingers. "Now. Out the window."

Parkman ran the other way and entered the bathroom, leaving the door slightly ajar.

"Dammit," she whispered under her breath. "Now you're going to get shot. You should've listened, Parkman."

The light in the bathroom was off, Parkman virtually unseen.

"Come in," Sarah called.

The door opened, and Father Adams stepped in.

"Ahh, Father Adams. How good of you to come. But you

must have the wrong room. No last rites needed here."

"Actually, I've come to talk with you about a small matter."

He kicked the door shut and turned to face her.

Chapter 24

HIRST WAITED IN FATHER Adams's office as instructed. The man of God was late for their meeting, but Hirst didn't mind. It gave him a chance to learn more about the priest.

At the door, he peeked out into the church. One woman sat in a pew by a statue of Jesus at the front, her eyes closed. Another woman sat near the back in the mostly empty pews, a Bible in hand.

He closed the office door, walked around Father Adams's desk, and opened drawers, rifling through paperwork and reading what he could. After five minutes, he realized he wouldn't get too far this way. He would need Adams's cooperation or a warrant to dig deep and determine who had access to church vehicles and property.

At Sarah's accident scene, they had secured the perimeter and searched each parking level one at a time. They found the vehicle involved in Vicky Chard's murder and Sarah's fall from the fifth floor. Inside the white van, they had found a snake cage. But there was no perp.

Something about Father Adams bothered Hirst: a self-assuredness, a smugness. How he became the church-appointed man to work with the police on the priest murders was something else Hirst wanted to know.

And what happened to his ear?

Hirst's cell phone rang.

"Hirst here. What's up?" He walked around the desk and sat in one of the visitor chairs.

"Detective Hirst, it's Robert Kellman. I'm one of the men assigned to talk to local businesses by the building where Vicky—"

"I know who you are. Why are you calling me?"

"I thought you'd want in on this right away."

There was a moment of silence on the line.

"This better be good," Hirst said. "Speak fast."

"Two stores up from the building where Father George was found, we have a security camera with video footage of the front sidewalk."

"And?"

"The store owner has given it to us."

"I'm assuming you watched it, or you wouldn't be calling me."

"Yes, sir, I did."

"And?" Hirst ran a hand through his hair.

"Sir, as far as I can tell, Father Adams, the man I saw at the crime scene the other night, is the same man walking a young girl into the building. He used a key at the front door."

"How sure are you?" Hirst asked.

"It's him because I saw him again."

"When?"

"On the camera."

Hirst held his breath for a moment, then blew it out. He got to his feet and left the office.

"What was he doing on the camera the second time?" he asked calmly.

"He walked Father George inside the building. This time I saw his face up close as it passed the camera. I followed his path to the front of the building, where he pulled keys, inserted them, and entered with Father George. There's no doubt, sir."

"Have you told anyone else about this?"

The woman in the front pew opened her eyes and glared at Hirst. He ignored her and kept walking to the street where his car was parked.

"No, sir. Called you first."

"Okay, call it in. Ensure everyone knows that Father Adams is a person of interest in this case."

"Got it," Kellman said.

Hirst dropped his phone into his pocket as he made it to the front of the church, slapped the door open, and ran for his car.

He needed to get to the hospital a few blocks away to warn Sarah and Parkman. There was a possibility that Adams wasn't through with her yet.

Chapter 25

Sarah released her grip on the fork and rubbed her face. Vivian had to get better at sending Sarah feelings or premonitions. Sure, someone was coming at any minute, but Father Adams was hardly a threat.

He moved across the room silently, his long coat draped past his knees, a brown fedora on his head. At the window, he stopped to stare down.

Sarah glanced at the bathroom door quickly. It still sat ajar with no sign of Parkman, who evidently was taking her warning seriously by staying hidden.

"What can I help you with?" Sarah asked.

She adjusted herself. Aches and pains populated her body, centering on her abdomen where the bruising had turned into a purple and black mess. How she got out of that car alive was still a mystery. The initial pain from being shot in the foot was the smacking vibration of the bullet. When she thought the foot had numbed, she had felt nothing because the bullet had done no harm.

He looked at her sidelong. "What faith are you?"

She narrowed her eyes. "How is that relevant?"

"Curiosity."

"I believe in God. Isn't that enough?"

He looked back out the window. "I'm not here to convert you—"

"Good."

"Since you're helping the police with the investigation and found yourself in trouble last night, I just wondered what you get out of all this."

"Redemption."

Adams's eyebrows rose, crinkling the skin on his forehead, but he didn't turn completely toward her.

"How's that?"

"I'm sure there's something more interesting to discuss, Father. Let's get on to that subject. Why are you here? Not that I have a problem with your visit, per se, but you came for a reason, yes?"

"I did," he mumbled. "I did." He cleared his throat. "How is it you're qualified to help the police?"

"They haven't told you?"

"I want to hear it from you." Father Adams turned from the window and sat in the chair Parkman had been in moments before.

"I have a special ability to track and hunt down the bad guys." She smiled. "Since I was almost killed roughly eight hours ago, I can have a sense of humor about it, no?"

"If you wish." He leaned back in his chair. "Tell me something else."

Sarah waited.

"Are you aware of the irony of you being here?"

After thinking about it a moment, Sarah couldn't come up with what he might be referring to.

"The look on your face," he said, "tells me you're unsure what I'm talking about." He slipped a hand inside a pocket on his jacket. "I'll ask the question a different way."

Sarah lowered her hand and gripped the fork again. Something about Father Adams had changed.

"The Bible discusses people who see the future and listen to the dead. It says they are practitioners of witchcraft. The Bible says you're working for the devil. Do you feel you're working for the devil and what you do is witchcraft?"

"If it is, I wouldn't stop. Because in the end, I get the bad guys, which is important. But I don't have a lot of faith in your Bible, and I don't believe in Satan, so I'm good."

He looked surprised. "Interesting. Your beliefs serve your purpose."

"Not exactly. My beliefs are facts, as I don't just feel the other side and channel my sister's messages. I have recently been able to feel her memories and be a part of her existence. That gave me an understanding of what is waiting beyond our mortal experience."

"And the Bible is worthless? Is that what you're saying?"

"Absolutely not. The Bible is filled with a ton of wisdom. It has served to help more people than not. But nothing in it holds up to scrutiny. Something as simple as the names of the Apostles—Paul, John, Matthew, Andrew, James—gave it away for me. How did they find guys with those names in the Middle East?"

Father Adams nodded slightly. "There are answers to

your questions, but I feel you're not interested in hearing them." He got up from the chair. "I've come to tell you that you're no longer needed in this investigation. Because you're a charlatan who claims to speak with the dead, which is anti-everything the church stands for, I can't allow you to work with the church in saving the lives of men of God."

"Is that the irony you spoke of?"

"You are hereby terminated from assisting the police," he said, ignoring her statement.

"I think you should wag more."

"Excuse me?"

"You're used to being up on the pulpit and preaching. Just wag more."

"I don't understand."

"Bark less, wag more. You'll keep friends that way."

He started for the bed.

Chapter 26

DETECTIVE HIRST DROVE HARD but kept the siren off. He had slowed at two red lights but preceded the green when he could.

Parkman's cell number kept going to a machine. He got no answer when he tried the officer on duty at the hospital.

Still three blocks from the hospital, he thought about dialing their main desk. Still, he would already be there by the time he called information, got connected with reception, and waited to be rerouted to hospital security.

Earlier, when Hirst was talking to Parkman in Sarah's room as she slept, Parkman received a call from a guy named Aaron. They had chatted for a minute, and then Parkman hung up. Hirst knew Parkman had his cell phone and that he was answering it. He either turned it off so Sarah could sleep, or there was a problem.

Hirst pushed the pedal to the floor, felt the cruiser jerk

forward, and decided to hit the siren.

Something bad was happening. He could feel it.

But would he be too late?

Chapter 27

As Father Adams approached the bed, he was close enough to see the bandage on his right ear that the fedora had mostly hidden.

Sarah met his eyes, everything coming clear in that instant.

Father Adams was the man from last night. Vivian had been right. Adams had inserted himself into the investigation and gone to the scene of the crimes. The scene of *his* crimes. Because she had psychic abilities and was getting close to him, he had to break from killing priests to take out the girl, the possessed girl who talks with the devil.

She wrapped her fingers around the fork and held it in a strike position under her leg.

"Doubting your faith?" she asked.

He pulled his hand out of his pocket, fingers wrapped around a gun. Before he could point it at her, she lunged with the fork, jerking across the bed in such a sudden movement that she screamed out at the pain from her ribcage.

Father Adams hopped out of the way, lowered the gun, and clicked off the safety.

Sarah rolled the other way, intent on dropping off the bed on the opposite side. She dreaded the thought of smacking into the floor but dreaded the thought of another bullet hole even more.

The gun fired as she crested the edge of the bed. She hit the floor hard, and the air was forced out of her lungs.

She ground her teeth at the pain but didn't stop moving. A quick spin of her shoulders and she rolled under the bed. Frantic to stay away from the gun, she watched for his feet.

Where's Parkman?

Adams walked around the bed to where she had fallen, but she wasn't there anymore.

Parkman?

Adams took two steps along the side of the bed and then stopped. Like a one-eyed snake, Adams pushed the weapon under the bed, searching for her.

Ignoring the pain in her chest and ribs, she jabbed the fork into the meat at the top of the hand that held the weapon. Father Adams cried out, and the gun pulled back.

A second set of feet appeared behind Adams's as he moaned at the fork still in his hand.

Parkman.

Someone was choking. She rolled out from under the bed and looked up as Parkman held Father Adams in a tight neck hold.

The hand with the gun, the fork still in it, blood seeping from the stab wound, rose. Adams aimed over his shoulder, backward at Parkman, who ducked his head aside.

The bullet tore into the bathroom wall, missing Parkman. Parkman yanked back so hard on Adams's neck that Father Adams's feet left the floor momentarily, but his gun hand persisted.

Before Sarah could get up on her one good foot, Adams brought the weapon down and twisted it behind him, turning the gun to aim at Parkman's midsection.

Adams fired.

Parkman jerked as if he'd been punched in the stomach.

Sarah screamed and dropped back to the floor, momentarily weakened by what she had just witnessed.

Parkman let go of Father Adams's neck and stumbled backward, his hands trying to keep the blood in as it seeped past his fingers.

Sarah had a crazy thought about being shot in a hospital and how he didn't have to go far to see a doctor.

She pivoted on the floor, brought up her good leg, and kicked the back of Adams's knees before he could turn toward her. Adams buckled but caught himself on the edge of the bed.

Parkman bumped the night table on his way to the floor and swung his arm wide, knocking the lamp down beside Sarah before hitting the floor himself.

As Adams faced her, his breathing haggard, he swung the weapon around. She grabbed the lamp Parkman had knocked over and brought it down on Adams's foot.

The gun went off again.

Chapter 28

DETECTIVE HIRST RAN INSIDE the hospital doors and stopped at security as the alarm sounded throughout the building. The guard was just getting off his chair as Hirst produced his ID.

"What's happening?" Hirst asked.

"Not sure," the overweight guard said as he donned his hat and started up the hall. "The buzzer is going off, and no one told me anything. No one ever tells me anything."

"What floor?"

"What?"

Hirst tried to stay calm. "Does the alarm tell you what floor the trouble is on?"

"The second floor."

Just then, the cop who was supposed to guard Sarah's hospital room door on the second floor came strolling down the hall toward them. He had a burrito or something like it in his hand, a piece of foodstuff on the corner of his mouth.

"Why aren't you at Sarah's door?" Hirst shouted.

"I was given a break."

"By whom?" Hirst shouted back.

"Father Adams came and said he'd stay with her for a while."

Hirst ran for the stairs. The cop and the hospital security guy followed him close. They hit the stairs running, one after another.

Hirst wanted to turn around and kick the cop's teeth in. If something had happened to Sarah or his friend Parkman, maybe he would do just that.

Before opening the door to the second floor, Hirst pulled his weapon and turned to see if the cop had his out, too.

"Drop the fucking burrito," he said softly but loud enough to be heard over the alarm. "The alarm is Sarah's room. Pull your weapon. Be ready."

"How can you be so sure it's Sarah's room?" the cop asked.

The security guard nodded. "Yeah?"

"Because Father Adams is our only suspect in the priest killings."

"What? Nooo …" The cop shook his head.

"And he's in Sarah's room."

"That would mean he killed Vicky last night and tried to kill Sarah in that parking garage—"

Hirst cut him off. "And he's trying again right now."

The cop pulled his weapon and nodded that he was ready.

Hirst opened the door to the second-floor hallway.

Chapter 29

THE NIGHT TABLE LAMP didn't damage Adams's foot much, but it was enough to knock off his aim. The last bullet he fired took a chunk from the floor beside Sarah's head.

Losing strength fast and in pain, Sarah spun away from him and rolled back under the bed. She kept rolling until she came out the other side, where she sat up. He would be on her at any second, and without a weapon, she would die in this hospital room. She was losing this fight fast and knew it.

He was already coming around the bed, the black hole of the barrel leveling at her. She was never one to give up, so she grabbed the empty juice glass on the end table and threw it at him.

He ducked and stepped back, giving her the break she needed to pull herself up and hop toward the window.

Someone knocked on the door. It must've given him pause because he didn't fire into her back. Near the window, she lost her balance on her weakened leg and dropped into the chair Parkman had sat in.

More knocking on the door.

Come in, dammit! It's not locked.

Adams crowded her, both hands fisted up.

Where's the gun?

Sarah flailed hard, trying to get a shot at him, but he hulked over her, maneuvering out of reach. Quick on his feet, he stepped in and delivered two hits to her chest and stomach. Her ability to fight was greatly reduced as he pounded on wounds caused by the airbag. Breathing became a chore. Coughing through each breath was difficult and painful, and trying to repel the attack was nearly impossible.

His fist connected with her jaw. Then her forehead. She collapsed in the chair and started to slide out of it, her eyes fluttering closed.

The floor meant death. Going down in this fight meant staying down.

Summoning the will to stay upright through the drowning-inside-her-own-body feeling tested her stamina.

Another of his hammer fists smacked her in the side of her head, the ear taking the hit. Then another slightly above the temple.

More knocking on the hospital room door. Someone shouting.

Parkman still bled in the corner.

She struggled to keep her eyes open as blood poured from old cuts opened on her forehead, bandages on her face torn off and askew.

She slipped off the chair toward the floor like a warm Jell-O. Adams's crotch was right in front of her.

Something heavy slammed into the door.

Her consciousness wavered for a brief instant.

His knee came up to meet her face. She had enough street-fighting experience to bob away from the impact of the knee. As she did that, her right hand shot out with a last bit of will to fight. It closed around his scrotum, and Sarah squeezed, locking her hand into a vise grip.

Father Adams let out a high-pitched wail and tried to step away from her, but Sarah allowed gravity to bring her all the way to the floor without letting up on her grip.

The door banged again like someone was body-checking it.

Just come in already.

Adams punched and smashed at her forearm in an attempt to dislodge her, but she refused, ignoring the pain and tightening her grip. His balls would burst in her hand before she let go and die.

The door whipped open, smacking the wall behind it.

She squeezed tighter.

Father Adams was close enough to the bed that he bent over, grabbed his gun, and brought it up to bear on the newcomers.

She thought about Aaron. She needed more training. This was too dangerous without the proper skills. Even with two broken feet, Aaron would've subdued this guy in half the time.

A gun went off. A second shot. A third.

Father Adams stepped away slowly, not jerking and pummeling at her like seconds before.

She lost the last bit of strength she had and released his scrotum. Others were here now. They could handle it. Sarah rested her head back and forced her eyes open as she wiped away the blood.

Father Adams had Parkman's or Sarah's blood on him as he pinwheeled his arms toward the room's window.

His gun came up, a horrid expression on his face.

Another weapon fired in the room again and again. Tiny eruptions formed in his shirt. He stumbled back as the glass in the window busted out from a bullet.

One second, Father Adams was there, covered in blood, a gun in his hand, the next second, he fell backward out of the hospital room window.

As Sarah lost consciousness, she understood it wasn't Parkman's or her blood on Father Adams's chest.

It had all been his.

Chapter 30

"It's over," a man said.

Sarah opened her eyes, though it took immense effort.

Why are my eyes so heavy?

She blinked a couple of times, wiped them, and then opened her eyes as far as she could.

Detective Hirst sat in a chair beside her bed.

"Parkman," she whispered. "How is he?"

Hirst set the magazine he'd been reading down and leaned forward in the chair, resting his elbows on his thighs.

"He'll be fine."

She closed her eyes. "How bad?"

"Gutshot. Missed anything vital. An inch from the spine. The bullet was removed without a problem. He's all stitched up and sleeping, recovering."

"How long have I been out?" She tried to open her eyes again but then gave up.

"Eighteen hours. They gave you a little something to sleep."

"Oh, that's what it is."

"What, what is?"

"Nothing. Am I cool? More injuries or less?"

"I didn't know it was possible, but you've got bruising on top of your bruises. You put up quite a fight at the end."

"Father Adams? Where is he?"

"Dead."

"How?"

"I shot him. He fell through the window."

"Did he hit the ambulance under the window?"

There was a pause before he said anything. "How did you know an ambulance was parked there?"

"I had Parkman look before Adams arrived."

"Oh."

"Weird luck, eh? Shot in a hospital room and smashed into an ambulance. I mean, who goes out like that?"

"Men of God."

"Supposed men of God. The guy was a murdering fraud."

"You should get more rest."

"I'm almost asleep now."

"One more thing."

"What?"

"Aaron's coming to visit. He'll be here when you wake next."

"Shit."

"Problem?"

"Don't want him to see me like this ..."

Her mouth stopped and hung open as she fell back under

the warm spell of the drugs in her system.

Chapter 31

THE FOOD WAS EQUALLY good as before. This time someone had splurged, and the hospital was taking her order. Maybe Detective Hirst had pulled a few strings. Sarah wondered if Parkman was getting the same deal.

Her abdominal bruising had turned a yellowish purple, and most of the minor aches and pains had subsided. Her broken foot was still healing nicely, and the wounds on her face were clearing up. Only her cracked rib protested when she moved or coughed, but something stronger than Advil kept it at bay.

It had been four days, and they were releasing her in the morning along with Parkman. Aaron had set up a hotel room for them as they wanted to stay for Father Adams's funeral tomorrow. A large congregation was set to commemorate the man's place with the church and the legacy he had left behind.

Because it would only hurt the Catholic church's relationship with the local authorities in an already stressed environment, the powers that be requested that Father Adams be buried without being named the priest killer. The police would spend an extra week filling in reports and closing files. Once the man was in the ground, the LAPD could release a sanitized version of what they had on the case and announce that the killings were over. They would say the case was closed and the suspect's body had been located. The city could rest easy as the police had done their job.

Sarah didn't like it at all. More cover-up, enabling and condoning, exactly how the Vatican preferred it. For Sarah, this tragedy cheapened the lives lost and the people hurt. But the church was a business just like any other. Revealing the truth could be looked upon as a smear campaign. The Vatican released financial statements showing their 2012 profit to be over a hundred million dollars. It appeared nobody wanted to rock that boat.

Someone knocked.

"Come in."

The door opened, and Parkman was pushed in on a wheelchair, Aaron behind him.

"Parkman's telling me you're quite the fighter with one foot," Aaron said.

"Parkman lies."

"No, no, he said the guy had a gun on you, and you still fought back with vim and vigor."

"That's what he called it?" she asked, smiling at Parkman as Aaron pushed him closer. "Vim and vigor? It's not that. It's a little something I call survival. What Parkman failed to say is that he's the one who can fight. He's the one who attacked the guy and almost finished him off."

"Let's just agree that we got lucky," Parkman said.

Aaron rolled him up to Sarah's bedside, where Parkman took her hand.

"You doing good?" he asked.

She pulled her hand away. "Better than you. And no coddling."

"Come on, Sarah," Aaron said. "Be nice. He took a bullet for you."

"Aaron, you want nice. Come over here. I'll give you nice."

"Whoa, you're not in any shape—"

"Fuck shape. Get over here."

Aaron did as he was told.

Smart man.

He crawled up on the bed beside Sarah and gently wrapped an arm around her. They kissed.

"I'm glad you're okay," he said.

"Me too," Parkman interrupted. "I'm still here, guys."

"We know," Sarah said without breaking eye contact with Aaron. "We just love each other, and I don't get enough of this in my day-to-day life."

"We love each other," Aaron repeated.

"Is that a question?" Sarah asked.

"Well, it's just, it kinda helps with what we're doing here. You know, being together and shit."

"Yeah, I guess love helps that along."

They smiled. Then giggled.

Parkman laughed as they kissed again.

Sarah winced in pain and pulled back, a hand rushing to her head. An image of Father Adams had filled her mind. The image was so sharp and clear that it came across as a short headache. She closed her eyes tight and winced.

"What is it, Sarah?" Aaron asked. "A headache?"

"You could say that."

"Can I get you something?" Aaron rolled off the bed. "You want a nurse?"

"No, no more nurses. Take me to the hotel. Let's have dinner. I want out of this place."

The image came again. But this time, it came with a message whispered into her inner ear. For a brief second, her eyes widened. It couldn't be. None of it was true. But Vivian was never wrong.

"Parkman?" Sarah said, her voice serious enough that both men turned to look at her. "Did you see the body?"

"Father Adams?"

"Yes."

"I saw him get shot over half a dozen times and leave your room backward out the window."

"But you didn't see the body?"

"What's this all about?" he asked.

"I was at the police station and talked to Detective Hirst," Aaron added. "He had just come from the autopsy room when I met with him. Hirst saw the body. That's for sure. Why do you ask?"

"I don't know," Sarah said. "It's weird."

"You're not making sense," Parkman said. "What is it?"

"Aaron, take us to the hotel. On the way, I want you to call Detective Hirst and have him meet us at the hotel. I have a message for him."

"Okay, Sarah, what message?"

"It's not over." She sat up and slipped off the bed onto

her good foot.

"What's not over?" Parkman asked as he looked at Aaron.

"Father Adams. Something tells me it's not over."

"That's impossible," Aaron said. "He's dead."

Sarah spun to face him. "I don't question Vivian," she said too sternly. "If Vivian says it's not over, then it isn't. Get me to the hotel and make sure Hirst meets us there." She grabbed her crutch, winced as she placed it under her arm, and walked to the closet for her clothes.

Neither man tried to help her. She preferred it that way.

"Okay, we'll do it your way, but I don't understand it unless Father Adams had someone working for him."

"It could be." Sarah dropped the hospital robe and slipped a shirt over her bruised ribcage. "I don't know all of it yet, but what I can tell you is if Hirst doesn't act fast, hundreds of people will die very soon at the hands of Father Adams."

Aaron gasped. Parkman looked away.

"By the way, that includes us. We all die unless this gets fixed. We're almost out of time. Call Detective Hirst. And let's roll."

Chapter 32

DETECTIVE HIRST HATED THE paperwork but understood it came with the job. That didn't mean that when the paperwork was complete, he couldn't rejoice. Getting out of the office by two in the afternoon, his recent case closed and no new cases to look at until next week, he could spend the rest of the day at home and then get up tomorrow to attend Father Adams's funeral, the publicly respected individual, but a privately hated one as well.

He pulled into his driveway and killed the engine, anticipating time with his wife. No work, no papers, no criminals, and no dead bodies. Just one gorgeous woman with needs that he was happy to fulfill. He knew what it meant to be married to a cop. He knew the long hours weren't conducive to a solid relationship. When he got these opportunities, he seized them.

He retrieved his briefcase from the backseat and then

stopped. After one look at the house, he decided his work wasn't coming home with him today. He popped the trunk and tossed the case in. Slamming the trunk lid, closing the car doors, and hitting the lock button on the key fob felt final. Today was Wife Day.

He strolled up the walkway, Janice on his mind, easing away thoughts of the past week. No lights were on when he opened the front door. He placed his keys on the stand beside Janice's, unclipped his holster, and set his gun in the locked cabinet underneath. The lock clicked when he closed it.

He straightened, pulled his pants up, and shouted, "Janice? Where are you?"

No reply.

"Janice?"

He started down the hall, looked in the living room, then the den, and ended up in the kitchen.

Maybe she's having a nap.

"Janice?" he called one more time, then realized that if she was napping, he didn't want to wake her. He took the stairs slowly, avoided the one that creaked, and made it to the second floor as a yawn escaped his lips.

Maybe he would nap with her. Sounded like a good idea after a busy week.

But their bedroom was empty.

He scratched his head and whispered, "Where is she?"

Her house keys were inside, sitting on the stand by the door. The front door had been locked. She was either in the house, in the backyard, or at a neighbor's place. He looked out the bedroom window. The lawn chairs were where they had always left them. No sign of her.

"Janice?" he called out as he stopped at the top of the

stairs.

Something thumped from below. He looked over the railing.

Instinctively he reached for his holster, but it wasn't there. His eyes wandered to the cabinet by the front door. Then the table with the keys.

He waited.

The house remained silent.

He started down the stairs, debating whether to put his holster back on. At the bottom, he decided against it. Too paranoid. This was his house. The priest killer was dead. It was over. No one would be here but Janice. The crime rate in this neighborhood was very low. With no signs of forced entry, and no outward signs of a struggle, Janice was okay, and he'd find her at any moment.

"Janice?"

The thump came again.

This time it sounded like it came from the basement. He turned that way. The basement door sat open about three inches. They never left it ajar. Janice was in the basement. It made total sense. No wonder she couldn't hear him calling her.

He walked over, pulled the door open all the way, and almost jumped out of his pants as his cell phone rang.

He fumbled for it and stepped back from the basement stairs.

"Yeah?" he blurted. "Who's this?"

"Aaron Stevens."

"Who?"

"I'm with Sarah and Parkman."

"Okay, what's up?"

"We've got trouble."

He stared at the open door, the stairs descending to darkness, an eerie feeling rinsing his stomach. "What kind of trouble?"

"Father Adams is dead, but it's not over."

"How's that?"

"We don't know just yet. Sarah wants you to meet us at the hotel. She'll fill you in there."

"When?"

"Now."

"Can't it wait?"

"Hold on."

Hirst listened as Aaron pulled the phone away and spoke to someone, the mouthpiece covered. Then he came back.

"No, it can't wait. Meet us within the hour and tell no one about this, or hundreds of people will die. According to Sarah, our window of opportunity is closing fast. Within hours, there will be nothing we can do to stop this. Hirst, just meet us at the hotel. We're in room 444."

"All right, I'll be there in half an hour, but Adams is dead, and the case is closed. I can't imagine what Sarah must be talking about, but—"

"Room 444. Just be there."

Aaron hung up.

Hirst pocketed his phone.

At the top of the stairs, he called his wife's name. Briefly, he looked back at the gun cabinet, entertained the idea of fetching his weapon, shook his head at the silly notion, and started down the stairs. At the third step, he flicked on the light.

Nothing happened.

He tried the switch two more times. Still nothing.

"Janice?" he said, his voice less sure, more cautious.

Maybe she fell while changing the bulb. Or maybe she tried to navigate the stairs and fell into darkness.

He pulled his cell phone out and turned on the flashlight feature. Using it to guide him down the rest of the stairs, Hirst got to the basement floor, swung the light around, and headed for the other light switch that turned on the part of the basement under the living room.

That switch worked.

And he saw Janice.

He almost dropped to his knees, but he'd been to enough crime scenes to remain on his feet. Only this one was personal. It was Janice, his Janice.

As he walked over to her, he asked all the usual questions. Who could've done this? Why did they do it? How did they do it?

Janice's hands were suspended above her head, tied to the unfinished basement's wooden ceiling. She was suspended, so her feet barely contacted the ground.

Hirst's stomach revolted, and he gagged, breathing deep to keep the contents down. He took a couple of extra deep breaths even as his eyes watered at what his brain was trying to comprehend.

Janice was naked except for a stained pair of white panties. Blood covered most of her body, and her face looked like a thousand bees had stung her. Her lips were swollen to twice the size, and her eyes were virtually swollen shut. Purple bruises covered most of her flesh, and she bled in more than ten spots where someone had taken a small knife, like an X-Acto blade, and made tiny cuts. Not enough to kill, but enough to cause great pain.

"Why?" he said out loud as he felt for a pulse.

A thick plastic black collar was wrapped around her neck. He pulled on it and then leaned in close for a better look.

"I wouldn't do that if I were you," a voice said behind him.

Detective Hirst spun on the balls of his feet, ducking his head, his hands coming up in a defensive posture.

Father Adams stood under the light, the shadow of his fedora covering one side of his face.

"You!"

"You see this?" Father Adams held up what looked like a remote control for a TV set. "This red button can be pressed from anywhere at any time, and that collar around your wife's neck will explode, effectively slicing her head clean off."

"What are you talking about?" Hirst said as he straightened up and took a step toward Adams.

The priest withdrew a gun, clicked the safety, aimed at Hirst, and fired the weapon. The bullet took a chunk out of the basement floor less than a foot in front of Hirst, then ricocheted once and came to a stop somewhere with a solid thunk.

"Are you fucking crazy?" Hirst gestured with both hands. "What do you want?"

"What everyone wants."

"And what's that?"

"Equality."

"Come again."

"This isn't the time. Let's talk about something a little

more pressing, shall we?"

Hirst waited for Adams to speak as sweat rolled into his eyes. He blinked it away.

"Detective Hirst. Walk around behind your wife, please."

"What are you, a magician? I mean, how did you do it? I saw your body on the autopsy table."

"That wasn't my body. Now, just walk around behind your wife." Adams raised the gun and pointed it at Hirst.

Hirst did as he was told, wishing he had gotten his gun in the cabinet after all. "Then whose body was it?"

"My brother, Mike. He was always a little less organized than I was. Messier. Working with him for these murders was an exercise in futility. I had a feeling his death was coming. But that doesn't matter as I will be dead very soon as well. Do you see the digital timer on my little device?"

Hirst examined his wife's neck. He pulled Janice's hair aside and saw the small red digits counting down from thirty hours.

"Yes," he said. "I see it."

"The collar around your wife's neck is timed to detonate tomorrow at six in the evening. I will be dead by four in the afternoon. That will give you two hours to bring your bomb squad over and remove the collar after I have deactivated it. Do you understand what I have told you?"

"Yes, but how will you deactivate it? If you can, then just do it now."

"How I turn it off isn't important. But what is of great importance is that you understand my instructions as I give them to you."

Hirst stared at the priest for a moment, then nodded.

"Good. Sit down."

He looked around for a chair.

"Sit on the floor by your wife's legs."

Hirst did as he was told.

"Listen carefully to what I need, and you and your wife will survive this little ordeal."

Surprised by his calm and clear head, he asked, "What did you do to her?"

"She let me in, we had tea, and we discussed you. Then she rooted around down here looking for her Bible. I simply offered her atonement for her sins. I was surprised at how sinful she has been. I'm sorry if she is in disrepair, but I assure you, it was necessary. She is still alive and will remain that way as long as you do what I want."

"And what is that?" Hirst asked. He adjusted himself and sat cross-legged. "What do you want?"

"I will be doing the eulogy tomorrow at my brother's funeral. Be there. And bring that girl Sarah Roberts and her friend Parkman. Listen to my eulogy with the rest of my congregation, and then I will die and be buried. Do this, and it will truly be over. You and your wife will be free."

"I was planning on being there anyway. You didn't have to do this."

"You were. But now that Sarah and Parkman are done in L.A., they may leave. Your wife's life depends on them being at the church. If they are not, I push this button." Adams pointed at the red button on the remote in his hand. "The collar is tamper-proof. If you attempt to remove it, your wife dies. If the time runs out, your wife dies. If Sarah and Parkman *don't* show up tomorrow, your wife dies. You can do nothing for her except what I tell you."

"How am I supposed to save her after we all come to the

eulogy?" Hirst wiped at tears. He didn't want to cry, but the thought of losing Janice—and the pain she must've gone through already at this maniac's hands—drove him nearly insane with anger and sadness.

"You'll have to trust me. Once the eulogy is complete, I will hand you this remote and explain how to deactivate the collar. There is a way, and only I know how. In the unlikely event that I die before tomorrow mid-afternoon, Janice will die, too. Please don't be stupid, Mr. Hirst. Do what is asked of you and tell no one of our arrangement. Nothing can stop Janice's death except you listening to my instructions."

Tears dripped down his cheeks. He wiped at them.

"Try to kill me now," Father Adams continued, "and your wife dies." Father Adams stepped backward, keeping his gun trained on Hirst. "I expect to see you tomorrow with Sarah and Parkman at church. It's been far too long, I'm sure."

Father Adams got to the stairs and paused.

"Any questions?"

How could Father Adams be alive unless he didn't attack Sarah in the hospital room? But the autopsy was performed on Father Michael Adams. There was no doubt. That left the notion of identical twins.

Father Adams had to be a twin. But a twin that no one knew anything about?

"You're examining your options?" Adams shook his head back and forth. "Tsk, tsk, tsk. There is only one option here. The only way out of this is to have everyone attend the church tomorrow. When my eulogy ends, I free your wife, and then I die. You won't get the chance to arrest me. That is all I can offer you."

Father Adams headed up the stairs.

Detective Hirst bowed his head and wept. When he was done, he wiped his eyes and looked up at his unconscious wife's face. He had failed her. He had done this. He couldn't wake her because he would have to face her. It was better if she slept through the pain.

He unplugged the large freezer in the basement corner and pushed it toward Janice as quietly as possible. Then he grabbed a throw blanket and laid it across the white top of the freezer. Once he was ready, and the freezer was lined up, he slid it under his wife's dangling body. First, her knees, then her butt lay on the freezer. When it was completely under her, her body weight was no longer pulling on her hands. Then he used part of the throw blanket to cover her mostly naked body.

Without another look at her, he walked out of the basement.

At the front door, Hirst grabbed his holster, strapped it under his suit jacket, picked up his car keys, and locked the door on the way out.

Why did Father Adams have it in for Sarah and Parkman? What was their connection, and why use Janice as leverage to get them to the church?

A cop's wife was off-limits. Sarah, Aaron, and Parkman brought this on. They brought this to his family's doorstep. He was sure he would learn everything he needed in room 444.

But to make sure, he pulled out his cell phone.

It was time to call in a few favors.

Chapter 33

AARON PULLED THE MINIVAN into the parking space at the hotel. He turned to Sarah. "Do you need a hand?"

"Nope." Sarah opened her door, pulled her crutch out, and hopped down. She slammed the door behind her and started for the hotel lobby.

"Help Parkman," she called over her shoulder. "Let's go. We need to talk. I need to think. We're running out of time. I'll meet you two in the room."

She got to the elevators and rose to the fourth floor. Once inside the room, she sat in the plush chair by the window and waited, staring outside.

Moments later, Aaron helped Parkman through the door and eased him onto the couch. He winced but didn't utter a complaint. Aaron turned on the kettle, then sat opposite Sarah in the chair.

"Is Hirst on his way?" she asked.

Aaron nodded. "He's coming."

"We'll wait for him. I need to think until he gets here. I don't want to say everything twice."

"Tea or coffee while we wait?" Aaron asked.

"Coffee."

"Nothing for me," Parkman mumbled.

Aaron prepared the cups quietly.

"I need the hotel stationery," Sarah said. "When you're done over there, can you bring it to me? Vivian has a few things to explain, and I'm unsure how she wants to go about that."

Aaron tilted his head and looked at her. "Not sure? What does that mean?"

"You'll see shortly."

Parkman rested his head back on the couch and closed his eyes. Minutes later, Aaron brought her a cup of coffee and the notepad from the desk. He grabbed his coffee and sat down.

Nothing solid came to her immediately. Only the faint whisper of an idea. Like an echo calling through the trees, a hollow sound accompanied by a light breeze. Her sister's voice, the susurrations of her soul, her existence, her essence. What was once Vivian, the young girl, now an old soul on the other side, was a mature woman filled with pleasure and joy. The pain that came with Vivian, the loss, was something external, something she talked about but didn't actually feel anymore on the other side. Not like a memory bank, more like a memory vault, sealed away behind walls Vivian could travel through by thought.

Sarah had begun to feel Vivian's memories like her own, but they were still foreign enough to know the difference.

Someone knocked on the door. Her eyes popped open. Aaron jumped up to answer it. Parkman sat in the same spot, rubbing his eyes.

There was a feeling that something wasn't quite right.

Detective Hirst brought friends, but they remained hidden in the hallway. Hirst was angry. He wanted answers, and he knew more than what Aaron had said on the phone.

Aaron let Detective Hirst in the room. Sarah sipped her coffee, then she spit it back into the cup.

"It's cold, Aaron. Didn't you heat it up?"

"Sarah, you've been out for half an hour."

That surprised her, but she didn't show it. The paper in her hand was empty. This new way Vivian talked to her was so fresh that she wasn't sure what she was supposed to tell everyone. She had felt Vivian's pain locked away. A darkness so deep it swirled against its confines, injuring the vessel that contained it. Sarah had mentally stood near the vault that held Vivian's pain and was sure it would explode and cover her, but it didn't.

What the hell, Vivian?

"You want a coffee, Detective Hirst?" Aaron asked as he closed the door behind him.

Hirst ignored him. He moved into the center of the room, assessed Parkman, looked at Sarah, then back at Aaron.

"Why am I here?" he asked.

"You looked pissed," Sarah said.

"Why am I here?"

"To talk."

"About what?"

"Things."

"Stop fucking around," Hirst shouted. His face reddened,

and his eyes bulged for a second. "Why call me and drag me all this way to play games? Tell me what you have to tell me."

"What's got you all riled up?" Sarah asked. "We're the ones who got shot." She pointed at Parkman. "And rammed into the ground." She gestured at her face. "While being body-fucked by a snake. You invited us down here, and you're angry at us?"

"According to him," Hirst pointed at Aaron, "it's not over."

"Take it easy," Aaron said, stepping closer. "Lose the attitude. We're all friends here."

Hirst didn't want to anger Aaron because Hirst would get hurt, and Aaron would get arrested. Cops weren't in his good books after what happened to his sister Joanne a while back.

"Detective Hirst," Sarah said, "if you want to save your wife, sit down, shut your mouth, and listen to what I have to say."

All three men turned to stare at her. Comically, all three frowned and held their mouths open at the same time. Any reference to saving the wife was new to Parkman and Aaron. Just as new as it was to her.

"I don't know how I know that, but Janice, I think that's her name, could use our help. Would you agree?"

Hirst nodded and walked over to sit beside Parkman.

"I'm so confused," Hirst said.

"Me too," Aaron added.

"What's really going on?" Hirst asked as he rubbed his thighs back and forth.

"You've been through a lot, Detective. Why don't you tell us what happened at your house today? It'll help to come from you as I'm only getting snippets of it. I know it's supposed to be confidential, but Father Adams can't hear us here."

Hirst told them what happened and what Father Adams instructed of him.

"He had a brother," Aaron said. "That's crazy. All this time, two killers were acting as priests."

"Tell me something solid, Sarah," Hirst said. "Help me out here."

"What do you want to know?"

"What happened to your foot?"

Sarah looked down at the Robo boot and recalled being tied to a couch in the Rankins' house, held by a murdering cannibal.

"I understood you already knew some of what happened in Canada."

"I do, but I don't understand how your sister would direct you with all this information and allow you to be in harm's way."

Sarah understood what he was asking. Could she, with her celestial contact, work to make sure Janice was saved?

"You know my attacker in Canada was a cannibal?"

Hirst nodded.

"Had I driven into Kelowna and told the police that a cop's wife was a murderer who eats her victims, how much proof would I have? What if I told them I knew where the victim's bodies were? Could they execute a search warrant on the word of a mid-twenties American girl who had never been to Kelowna in her life?" She lifted her cold cup and gestured for Aaron. He grabbed it and began fixing her another coffee. "If all that panned out, would that cop, Barry

Ashford learn any lessons? Would he keep hurting girls at his massage parlor?"

"Okay, I get it. But you do this at great personal risk. You could've been killed."

"I could've been killed a thousand times by now, but I do this because I have to. I needed to go to Kelowna, piss that cop off, attack him, and expose him. He was so vile that even his own wife wanted him dead. Once she did that on camera and imprisoned me, all the evidence the authorities needed was easily collected. Sometimes things get a little out of hand, and I get hurt. Taking Barry and his wife off the streets is worth it. I can heal. And I don't believe Vivian would send me to my death. And even if she did, I would wake up on the other side and be able to slap the shit out of her for letting me die because, as a team, we're doing some good here."

Hirst looked like he was starting to relax. "Can you help my wife? If so, how?"

"We go to the church tomorrow and listen to the eulogy. But before doing that, we ensure all the emergency exits are unlocked and ready because I think Father Adams wants to go out in flames."

Aaron stepped back into the main room with Sarah's coffee. He exchanged a look with Parkman.

"Fire?" Aaron said. "Do you know anything else about his plan?"

"Just that he wants the three of us dead along with him."

"Great. That kinda sucks."

"I know. I'm not looking forward to it either."

Sarah looked to the side and stared at the wall for a moment. She turned her eyes to the carpet.

"What is it?" Aaron asked.

Slowly, she looked up and stared at Hirst. "You're wondering why Adams wants us at the church. You don't think we're telling you everything. In your mind, what he did to Janice is somehow our fault."

Hirst looked between Aaron and Sarah, then turned to Parkman.

"I've known you a long time, Parkman. I asked for help. I know I brought this on myself, but you assured me that she" —he pointed at Sarah, and Aaron moved in to deal with the offending arm, but Sarah waved him off—"that she was safe and that she didn't kill that cop in Canada. I should've listened to my colleagues. I should've never asked for her to come here."

"You were right in bringing Sarah," Parkman muttered. "Without her, this wouldn't be over. She led us to that building where you found Father George. She led us to the parking lot where Evelyn worked. And she will lead us through this till the end."

Hirst was shaking his head. "No, she won't." He got to his feet. "It ends here. It ends now. You three will come with me and tell us everything. When we're done, we'll bring you to the church tomorrow and find out what Father Adams wants to do. He will release my wife, and then he'll die as he said, or he'll go to prison for a very long time."

It was Sarah's turn to shake her head. "That doesn't work."

Aaron moved closer. He stood two feet from Hirst.

"You don't have a choice," Hirst said.

"Actually, I do. I have Aaron."

As if on cue, he stepped in behind Hirst, wrapped his arms under Hirst's armpits, brought his hands up, and interlaced them around Hirst's neck. In under seconds, Hirst was immobilized. When Hirst struggled and tried to kick backward, Aaron easily anticipated him and adjusted his hold to where Hirst shouted for him to stop.

"Tell your men to go home," Sarah said. "We've been honest with you from the beginning and are honest with you now. We can help, but your plan will get us all killed."

She detected a slight nod of his head.

Someone knocked on the door.

"Who is it?" Sarah asked, even though she already knew it was Hirst's backup.

"Room service. A Detective Hirst ordered coffee and teas brought up."

"We don't want any. Go away."

"I'm sorry, ma'am," the guy yelled through the door. "We have to hear it from Hirst. He'll need to sign for it."

Sarah nodded at Aaron. "Let him go."

Aaron's arms slipped out of the hold on Hirst in a flash, and the detective almost lost his footing. He collected himself, adjusted his jacket, and walked to the hotel room door.

When he opened it, three men in suits filed in. The front two pulled weapons and held them down by their legs.

"Is that your play?" Sarah asked. "Is that how you want to handle this?"

Hirst was obviously angry. His face had reddened from his ordeal with Aaron, and it maintained that hue as he shouted at Sarah. "I want to know why Father Adams tortured my wife, strung her up like a side of cattle, and placed a fucking bomb on her neck. Tell me everything, and you can go home. You can get out of my city. I'll clean it up my way."

Aaron hadn't moved. When Hirst was done shouting, he turned to Aaron. Hirst's hand came so fast it was a blur. But Aaron still managed to duck back and right himself, Hirst's hand completely missing. Hirst tried again, stepping into it, but missed again.

"Hold him!" Hirst shouted.

"You shouldn't do that," Sarah warned.

Two men stepped forward while the third raised his weapon at Aaron's face and shook his head back and forth quickly.

"Don't," the gunman said.

With one man on each side holding Aaron's arms, Hirst moved in until he almost touched Aaron's nose.

"I'm a fucking detective. You don't grab me and hold me like a common street thug. And since she's not talking and telling, I'll hurt you to get to her. Maybe then she'll tell us what we need to know."

The man with the gun lowered it once he saw Aaron was secure.

"Wait," Sarah said.

Everyone turned to her.

"Vivian's trying to say something."

They waited.

Sarah grabbed the pen and paper and laid her head back as if in a trance. She wrote something down, then snapped her head up and read the words.

"What did she say?" Hirst asked. "What's on the note?"

Sarah met Aaron's eyes and offered a slight nod. He understood what he was to do.

She held up the note. "Just two words. The first one is

fuck, and the second one is *you*." Sarah looked at Hirst. "I guess she means you."

Then she threw the pen at Hirst.

He blinked, but that was all Aaron needed. He bounced up and lifted his feet until they connected with Hirst's chest. When he pushed off Hirst's chest, the detective flew backward, and the two men holding his arms were knocked off balance. The man on Aaron's left arm connected with an end table and fell, releasing his grip on Aaron.

The second his arm was free, he swung at the man holding his right arm. One carefully measured hit, and the man gagged as his throat threatened to close. In the few seconds this took, the man who had previously held the gun on Aaron was still reacting, still raising the weapon when Aaron dove at him. They slammed into the wall as one, and the gun dropped safely to the carpeted floor.

Aaron lifted the man's legs, wedging the man's upper body between Aaron and the wall. With three other men in the room, two unhurt and ready to fight, Aaron had to act fast.

He released the man's legs. As the man fell to the carpet, Aaron dropped, retrieved the gun, slipped sideways in case someone was directly behind him, and landed on his back, the gun up and aimed.

The man who had toppled over the end table stood over him, fists at the ready.

"Back up," Aaron said.

"I'd do it," Sarah added. "Aaron doesn't like cops much. Compared to him, cops are my pals."

The man took a slow step back. The goon beside Aaron rolled away and got to his feet. Aaron did the same, keeping the weapon trained on them. The one who got hit in the throat was starting to breathe normally again.

"Everyone up against that wall," Aaron said.

They listened, moving as one, their hands raised slightly at the waist.

"Not you, Hirst," Sarah said.

He stopped and turned to her.

"Sit."

He sat.

While Aaron held Hirst's backup men against the wall by the door, Sarah leaned closer to Hirst.

"We still want to help. And I know how to free Janice. But you have to do it my way."

"Prove it. How can I trust your way? You were ready to leave the city. It was supposed to be over. But now Janice may die. So why should I trust you?"

"Aaron's arms are probably getting tired. Tell your men to leave the building. They can wait outside. If you don't like what I have to say, collect your men and do whatever you like. But for now, they can't be here."

Hirst thought about it for a moment. He looked at Parkman.

"We've got history, Hirst," Parkman said. "Come on, you know me. You may not know Sarah and Aaron, but you know me. Listen to what she has to say."

Hirst turned to his men. "Okay, it's over. There's nothing here. I'll meet you downstairs."

Two of them moved toward the door. The third one held back.

"I want my piece."

"Aaron?"

"Nope. Sorry. I'll give it to Hirst when he leaves, but not before. Or you can try to relieve me of it. I haven't broken any bones yet today. So, what's it gonna be?"

"It's fine, Baker. I'll bring your weapon down with me."

Baker moved along the wall to the open door and stepped out, mouthing a word under his breath.

Aaron wasn't petty enough to ask what he said. He just slammed the door behind the three men and set the night lock. Then he stood beside the door, the gun still in his hand, his back to the wall.

"You were saying?" Hirst said.

"Here's how we save Janice and still make it to the church on time."

When Sarah was done telling them everything, Hirst was the first to respond.

"How is it possible that you would know that much about my personal life? There were so many things you said that only I know about."

"I need you to trust me. I need you to know that I have access, through my sister, to vast amounts of knowledge. That's how I know how to fix this mess."

"Are you sure this'll work? You're sure that Janice's collar *isn't* a bomb?"

"I'm only as sure as Vivian is. It's her plan, her idea."

Hirst lowered his head. "I've known and trusted Parkman for a very long time. When I saw my wife today, all beat up and shit, I don't know, I just snapped." He looked up. "I mean, nobody does that to a cop's wife. And he said it was all because he needed you three at the church tomorrow."

"We were already planning on attending the eulogy. Although we didn't plan on it being read by Father Adams, though."

"To know the real reason why Janice was tortured, it just boggles my mind at how insane Adams is."

"Have we all got the plan, then?" Sarah asked.

Hirst nodded. "I've got it."

"Any chance we'll get another visit from your friends?"

"None." He turned to Parkman, who had stayed mostly quiet. They shook hands. "I'm sorry I doubted you and Sarah. I won't do it again."

He got up and moved to the door. Aaron handed him the gun, and Hirst gave Aaron a key to his house. Then he took one look back and nodded at Sarah and Parkman.

"See you tomorrow at the church around two in the afternoon."

Sarah nodded, suddenly very tired.

After Hirst left, Aaron secured the door and plopped down in the chair opposite Sarah.

"Are you sure about the collar on Janice?" he asked.

"No."

"What do you mean? She'll die if that thing really is a bomb."

"I know, but there's nothing we can do about it now. He will leave her alone until after the eulogy tomorrow. That's all I need."

"For what? What's actually going to happen tomorrow?"

Sarah thought about her answer and then said, "All I can tell you is that doing it Hirst's way would've gotten us, along with hundreds more, killed. Doing it my way minimizes the deaths to maybe a couple."

"Who might die?"

"Janice and me."

"Great. Just fucking great."

"But I'm still working on saving our asses. I just need to think. Vivian will help."

Aaron got up to pace the floor. "What are the odds you die?"

Sarah looked at Parkman, then Aaron, and said, "Don't ask me that. I don't like the answer."

Chapter 34

When Aaron parked in front of Detective Hirst's house, Sarah got her crutch, set it down, and stepped from the vehicle. Detective Hirst's car was nowhere to be seen, as they had discussed yesterday. If Father Adams had anyone watching the house, they would probably be gone by now. The eulogy was set to start in just over an hour.

Sarah entered through the kitchen door at the back of the house with the key Hirst had given Aaron. Quietly, she started across the kitchen but stopped at the sight of the knife block on the counter. She would need to cut through the ropes that secured Janice to extract her. Sarah selected a large knife and headed for the stairs to the basement.

One by one, she descended the stairs with her crutch carefully.

"Who's there?" a female voice asked from the depths of the basement.

"Janice?" Sarah said. "I'm a friend."

She had considered sending Aaron into the house for this part but realized it might spook Janice into thinking he was one of the aggressors.

"Who are you?"

"My name is Sarah Roberts. I'm here to take you to see your husband."

Sarah got to the bottom stair, the sun offering enough light through the small basement windows for her to have a partial view of the freezer Detective Hirst said he had placed under Janice.

Sarah moved inside the basement a little farther. Janice's hands were still tied above her head, pale in the small amount of light that reached them. Her face was spotted with blood and bruises contrasting with a blanched look, matching the freezer's complexion.

With the knife hidden behind her leg, Sarah said, "Janice, I'm here to help you leave this place. How are you feeling?"

Janice's eyes made furtive gestures over Sarah's shoulders as if looking for someone else in the room.

"I'm alone, Janice. Your husband sent me." Sarah stopped a couple of feet in front of Janice. "I'm going to untie you now, and together we'll leave. I will take you to your husband."

Janice shook her head fast, two quick shakes like she was in a hurry to deny Sarah's wish.

Tingling accompanied the hair rising on Sarah's neck as she felt someone step up close behind her. She was sure Father Adams would have someone watching Janice for such an eventuality.

Sarah waited for an extra breath, gripped the crutch tight

in her left hand, then dropped to her knees and swung it behind her.

The man anticipated her move and jumped over the crutch like skipping rope. When he touched the floor of the basement, his hands landed on Sarah's shoulders. He clutched her shirt, lifted upward, and then thrust it down. She hit the floor, not expecting the blow, and winced as her wounds ignited in pain. She curled into a ball, clenched at the agony in her ribcage while trying to see the face of the man who had crept up behind her.

He was a young-looking boy, maybe twenty years old. With a devilish grin on his face and a cell phone in his hand, he dialed out.

Sarah remained still for a few moments to think. Aaron was outside. When she didn't come out with Janice, he would come in to investigate. The kitchen door at the back of the house was still unlocked.

"Yes, Father, I know you're busy. But something has come up."

He paused to listen.

Sarah hadn't let go of the knife. An experienced fighter would've frisked her by now, relieving her of all weapons.

In an attempt to move closer to the boy, Sarah groaned and cried out, wincing as she moved. Now one of his polished black shoes was touching her right hip bone.

"Are you safe to talk now?" the boy said into the phone. After a pause, he said, "A girl named Sarah has just shown up to free that detective's wife." He waited. "Because she told the wife her name. That's how I know it." A longer pause this time. "Are you sure, Father? I will, Father, as long as it's not committing a sin. Yes, I understand. The Bible does talk about that. Yes, Father."

Sarah twisted toward his leg, bringing the kitchen knife around in a wide arc. The sharp blade connected with the side of his shin, slicing into his pants, then cutting through flesh.

He shouted and stepped away from her like he'd been stung by a bee. She swung again and again until she had sliced his pants four times. He lost his balance and fell straight back to the floor as if he was going to sit in a chair.

As Janice egged her on, Sarah got to her hands and knees and then lunged at the boy, the knife out front. She landed halfway up his body, the blade firmly pressed against his throat.

"Stop squirming," she shouted. "Do you have a death wish?"

The boy stilled under her.

"Who are you?" Sarah asked.

The boy's eyes watered, and his face reddened, but he didn't say anything. He just stared at her like she was evil incarnate.

"I don't have time for this. I'm going to get up now and untie that woman. Then we're leaving. The question is, what to do with you?"

He muttered something.

"Speak louder."

He uttered one word. "Alive."

Sarah eased back, pulling the knife along with her. As she did, she felt along his body with her free hand for hidden weapons.

Janice whimpered on the freezer behind them. Why hadn't she warned Sarah about the boy? Maybe he was the one who had tortured her, and if Sarah was unsuccessful, she didn't want to go through that again. It would make sense that Janice saw Sarah as a less-than-capable female with her broken foot and crutch.

Sarah got to her knees, retrieved the crutch, and stood up.

"Go on, get out of here," she said, smacking him with her crutch. "Get up."

The boy scrambled away on his elbows, pushing with his feet. He got up and disappeared in the shadows of the basement, leaving a small pool of blood.

Letting him go probably wasn't a good idea.

But time was elusive. She had to get to the church.

She hobbled over to Janice, applied the knife to the rope binding her hands, and sliced back and forth.

"He had a … gun," Janice whispered.

That sent a chill down Sarah's spine. When she turned around, they were still alone. She pulled her cell phone out to text Aaron. At the second she pushed the button to send the text, the sound of his phone receiving the text chimed from somewhere in the basement.

Aaron wasn't waiting in the van outside anymore. He was here.

Sarah moved to the other side of the freezer and continued slicing through the rope.

"Stay low," Sarah whispered. "Once your hands are free, move to my side and get down behind the freezer."

Janice nodded frantically.

Sarah sliced. A shoe scuffed the floor behind her. She ducked low and glanced over her shoulder. The boy had returned, a gun in his hand, raised and pointed at Sarah.

He strode across the floor to her. "You're an abomination," he shouted. "You defy our Lord and aid in the

Devil's bidding." He was nearly screaming now.

Sarah sliced the ropes faster.

"And you will go to Hell where you came from as our Lord God is my witness."

He stopped two feet from her, his finger twitching inside the trigger guard.

"I can't go to Hell because it's closed at the moment," Sarah said. "All the little devils are here, on Earth." She studied his finger, waiting for it to twitch, the biggest struggle going on inside the boy's religious-tainted mind. Would he kill another, something he was so staunchly against? How far had Father Adams brainwashed him? How far would an altar boy, if that's what he was, go for his master, his Father?

"Are you sure you should be out in public without your horns?" she asked.

She studied his trigger finger for movement while getting the blade ready to swing at the arm holding the gun.

Aaron eased out of the shadows four feet away. Like a club, Aaron swung his arm down across the top of the boy's elbows. Instantly, the boy's arms retracted, and the gun's aim went skyward. Aaron kicked at the back of the boy's knees. He folded and dropped to the ground. Then Aaron landed on him and locked his arms up, wrapping his legs around the boy's abdomen. In seconds, the boy was immobilized with no room to struggle.

Aaron met Sarah's eyes. "Carry on," he said.

Sarah turned back to Janice and attacked the ropes with the knife. Finally, the thick rope gave way, and Janice's hands were liberated. She dropped to the top of the freezer with a hard thud, then rolled to her side.

Sarah helped her up. "Can you walk on your own?" Sarah asked.

"What about this?" Janice pointed to her neck, where the explosive device was affixed.

"Oh, that's not a worry. The remote Father Adams showed your husband was a TV remote. It's an elaborate replica. This only looks like a bomb."

"How can you be so sure?"

"Someone very reliable told me. Let me have a look at that."

Sarah stepped in close and examined the black plastic collar. When she found the clasp, she clicked it and opened the lock. Then she pulled it safely from Janice's neck.

"See, no big deal."

"Whoa, that was scary." Janice held a hand to her rapidly moving chest.

"Agreed. Scary," Aaron said from the floor.

"You done down there?" Sarah asked. "We have a church to get to."

"Yeah, I guess so."

Aaron released his legs and let the boy's arms go. Then he grabbed the longest length of rope and secured the boy's wrists to a support beam. Once that was done, he jumped in the air and came down hard on the boy's right shin. The bone cracked.

The boy screamed a high-pitched wail.

Janice cringed. "Why did you do that?" she asked loud enough to be heard over the boy.

Aaron turned to her. "No one pulls a gun on Sarah without consequences. He had intended to shoot her. I broke his leg and tied him up because he needs to still be here when the police arrive."

The boy cried out, his head back as he screamed in pain.

Aaron looked down at the boy on the floor. "The police will be here soon. An ambulance will take you to the hospital, and they'll give you painkillers. Either before or after that, you'll be arrested for what you did here." He turned to the two women. "Let's go."

Sarah held out her hand. "Get his cell phone and his gun. I'll need both."

Aaron did as he was told and helped Janice get dressed and then out to the van. Once Sarah was in the passenger seat, he pulled away from the curb.

Sarah checked the boy's gun. It was fully loaded.

Then she called the police and told them what they would find in Detective Hirst's basement.

After hanging up with them, she checked the boy's phone to see what number the boy had called when he talked to Father Adams. The caller ID said Cane Father.

The traffic bunched up as they headed deeper into Los Angeles.

"Get us there as soon as you can, Aaron. Something terrible will happen if we're not there in less than half an hour."

Chapter 35

Sarah grabbed Aaron's cell phone and called Hirst. It rang once.

"Hirst here."

"It's Sarah. We got Janice. The collar's off."

"Oh, thank goodness." He breathed in deep over the line and exhaled. "Can you put her on?"

"Yes, but we need to talk after. Keep it short."

She handed the phone back to Janice.

"How much farther, Aaron?"

"Not much now. Five, maybe ten minutes."

"Okay, thanks, baby." She touched the side of his face. "Did I tell you I'm happy you're here?"

"Not yet, Sarah." He shook his head back and forth. "Nope."

"Okay, then I'll wait. Wouldn't want to make you feel that I've taken you for granted."

"Can't say that'll ever happen."

She pulled on his ear lobe gently, then turned back to Janice. "I need to talk to your husband."

Janice said goodbye and passed the phone forward to Sarah.

"Hirst?"

"Yeah?"

"While we deal with this church thing today, can you get someone to research Father Adams and his brother? I need to know where they were born, how they came to be in L.A., what investments they might have, do they have any other family locally, what bank accounts, etc. Anything you can find on these guys."

"Why's that? Where's this coming from?"

"I'm starting to feel that this isn't religiously based."

"What are you talking about? Is this coming from Vivian?"

She ignored the question. "Just learn as much as you can about their family's financial situation. Can you do that?"

"I'll set it up—"

The boy's cell phone in Sarah's lap began to ring. Call display said, Cane Father.

"Listen, Hirst, I gotta go. Just do it, and I'll see you at the church in five minutes or less."

She hung up on him and set Aaron's phone aside.

The boy's phone rang for the third time. She snuck a glance at Aaron. He nodded for her to pick it up.

She hit the answer button and said, "Hmm," deep enough to sound male.

"Is it done? Have you offered that Sarah woman her atonement?"

"And I thought you liked me," Sarah said in her high-school voice.

Father Adams's church came into view straight ahead. Suddenly an image of the entire church on fire smacked into her consciousness. She withdrew into her seat, her head resting against the back while she waited for Father Adams to speak again.

"Sarah Roberts. What have you done with my Ralph?"

"He's tied up at the moment. And in quite a bit of pain."

"Naughty, naughty, Sarah."

"I've been called worse."

"What possessed you to come to L.A. and attempt to ruin my plans? Oh, I know, the devil possessed you."

"Yeah, right, and you're about as religious as the sewer rat running around in the depths of your skull."

"Offering your own sermons now, are you?"

Aaron pulled over and double-parked the van. He killed the engine and jumped out.

"Only preaching to the preacher because I'm the one who gets to send you home. I'm the lucky one who gets to set up your meeting with God. He will decide your fate. But you, your time on this planet is over."

"I see it differently."

"Fire?" Sarah said.

She barely caught the audible intake of air on the other end of the line.

"Gotta go, asshole," Sarah said. "Got a madman to kill. See you soon."

She clicked off and dropped the phone in her pocket. Aaron opened her door. He handed her the crutch, helped her out, and shut the door behind her.

The three of them walked along the busy sidewalk. Up ahead, the police had cordoned off an area circling the church as the funeral attendance would be huge. A massive amount of people, probably more than they anticipated, constantly showed up to pay their respects to the late Father Adams.

At the yellow-tape line, an officer advanced on them, waving them back.

"We're here with Detective Hirst. Call him. He'll verify us. This is Janice Hirst, his wife."

The cop pulled out a cell phone, spoke briefly, then nodded at them.

"Come this way."

He pulled aside the barrier, let them in, and pushed it back in place.

They were escorted to the middle of the road, where a line of police cars were parked behind the hearse at the front of the church.

Parkman and Hirst came running over.

"Thank you, Officer," Hirst said, waving the man off.

Hirst grabbed Janice and hugged her.

"I thought I lost you," he said.

Parkman grabbed Aaron's shoulder. "No trouble?"

"Not really. One of Adams's boys tried to stop us. He's tied up in the basement, waiting for the police to come and arrest him."

Sarah studied the front of the massive church with its two spires rising into the sky on either side. The gray stones that made up the façade, the aged wood along the sides. The grass out front was manicured, and the magnificent stained glass offered the building its own character. The bell tower was the tallest point. From the front of the church, Sarah could see the large bells and wondered how they got those heavy beasts high up in an age before modern cranes and helicopters.

"Sarah?" Parkman said. "What are we doing here? What's the next move? Anything from Vivian?"

"Yes." She looked away from the church. Hirst and his wife stood side by side. With Aaron next to her, she had everyone's attention. "You're too close to the church," she told Hirst.

Parkman and Hirst looked at the building, then back to Sarah.

"How's that?" Hirst asked, his face impassive, pensive.

"When it blows, all these cars will be destroyed. They're in the debris field, and anyone this close will probably die."

Janice gasped while Parkman moved closer. "What are you talking about? He has explosives?"

"As far as I know."

"What does that mean?" Hirst asked. "You can't say shit like that without backing it up. As far as you know isn't good enough."

"Actually, it is good enough. Because when the place blows and people die, I can at least say that I warned you."

"Say I move everyone back and start emptying the church, and nothing blows up. What then? You wanna handle the press conference and explain your lack of reasoning?"

"Sure. I'll deal with the press. But where's this hostility coming from? I brought Janice back, didn't I? You can start trusting me now. Yesterday, in the hotel, you said you wouldn't ever doubt me again."

"Sure, I can trust you, but do they?" He pointed at the throng of people making their way inside the church. "Do you realize the kind of debacle it would create to evacuate the church now? It would be nearly impossible."

"Just make the call. Trust me. Do it now."

"Doesn't happen that way." Hirst turned to Parkman for support. "Tell her it doesn't happen that way."

"Sarah?" Parkman touched her arm. "What's going on? What's Vivian telling you?"

"Vivian isn't sure. Something's riding on it."

Hirst stepped into her space. "I can't order an evacuation on 'Vivian isn't sure.' You have no idea how bad that would look?"

"Sarah, what are you not telling us?" Aaron narrowed his eyes and frowned.

"I don't know," she said, leaning into his arms. Speaking only loud enough for Aaron and Parkman to hear as a couple of police cars drove by, she said, "Vivian's got a new way of talking to me. Handwritten notes are becoming a thing of the past. Ever since I got shot in the head, she's been whispering like she's trapped in a deep part of my consciousness. It's like I have two brains, and mine is the dominant one." She turned to Hirst, who was talking to his wife. "Hey, Hirst, to be safe, just order everyone out of the church. Just get as many people clear as possible. The people outside can take shelter if the building blows."

"Can't do that," Hirst said. "The church is crawling with cops. Logistical nightmare. Unless you have absolute proof."

"Then I'll do it," Parkman said as he started away.

"I'll join him," Aaron added.

"Wait!" Hirst called after them, but neither one turned back.

"Aaron!" Sarah called.

Aaron stopped, but Parkman kept going. She waved him

back. Hesitantly, he returned to her side.

"What is it?" he asked. "You want everyone out. I can help with that."

"I know. But I need you here."

"For what?"

"To help me in one minute."

"To do what?" he whispered, close to her ear.

"Follow my lead."

He gave her room, nodded slightly, and waited for her to do whatever she had in mind.

It had to be her going into the church. That was the only way. But would a church full of grieving parishioners and police officers listen to a wounded girl on a crutch?

Detective Hirst was now on a police radio telling someone to let Parkman in but to stay in the church. "Don't listen to Parkman," Hirst said. "Do not evacuate the church. Keep everyone looking for Father Adams. Make sure we don't miss the bastard."

The boy's phone rang in her pocket. Sarah pulled it out. Hirst was so close he bumped into her and looked down at the phone in her hand.

"Who's Cane Father?" Hirst asked.

"It's Father Adams. I found this phone on the boy holding Janice."

Hirst frowned, knowing he hadn't heard the whole story yet. "Why does it say Cane Father?"

"A religious version of a sugar daddy? Who knows."

"Hold on. Don't answer right away. Let me get my guys to set up a trace—"

Sarah clicked the answer button before he could finish. As if they were old pals, she said, "Hello there. Long time."

"I see you," Adams said.

"How nice. Do I look pretty? Are you coveting me? Which reminds me, how many commandments have you broken this week?"

"I don't adhere to that particular ideology. The church is a business. That's why I'm here. To make money."

"Tell it to someone who will listen to the rantings of a lunatic. I ain't got the time to play games." Hirst crossed his arms in front of her, evidently pissed that she didn't wait. She looked away from him. "Where are you, Adams? Come on. Give it up. Come dance with me."

"You will dance soon enough. In a lake of fire, demon. In the meantime, come join us inside. Church is in session."

"Sounds like a delightful invitation. But I'm feeling kinda woozy. I think I'll pass."

"If you don't enter the church to hear the eulogy for my brother, I will begin executing pedestrians and police officers."

"Oh, really? And how are you going to do that?"

"I've got snipers set up around the street. I push a button on cue, and they have orders to shoot. Orders to kill."

"Aren't you a religious man?"

"Absolutely. But so was Jim Jones in his own way. And how about Hitler? Wasn't he a great artist? He even made Time's Man of the Year in 1938. How about the president of the United States? Isn't he a man of religion? Yet he has snipers in his employ."

Sarah grabbed Hirst's attention and pointed skyward at the surrounding buildings. She covered the mouthpiece and whispered, "Snipers." Then she shrugged as if to say she wasn't sure Adams was bluffing.

"Religion doesn't come into it," Adams continued. "We are all human, and humans kill each other. We're at the top of the food chain. Nothing hunts us except ourselves. We'd have been overpopulated decades ago if we didn't have world wars. Humans are unique in that they have their own brand of population control, but that's another topic entirely." He paused. Sarah waited. "If you don't start for the church within one minute, I will execute a woman first. Then I will order someone killed every minute you remain outside. Start walking now."

The line went dead.

She glanced up at the church's spires, then the bell tower.

"What did he say?" Hirst asked, his face glistening with sweat.

"I've got one minute." She checked the time on the phone. "In fifteen minutes, it'll be four in the afternoon."

"What does the time have to do with anything?" Hirst nearly shouted, his confusion fueled by anger.

"At four, the church will explode." She met the detective's eyes. "At least that's what I think. That's why he wanted all of us here. This isn't about the Catholics like I previously thought."

"What's it all about, then?"

Sarah checked the time. Forty seconds had passed. If Adams weren't bluffing, someone would die in twenty seconds. She had to get inside the church if only to save lives on the outside. But she needed the church to be evacuated as fast as possible to limit Adams from seeing it.

"Aaron!" she called.

Now that she had his full attention, she withdrew the gun she had collected off the boy who had guarded Janice, wrapped an arm around Hirst's neck, and set the tip of the weapon against his throat. The crutch fell harmlessly to the concrete. His hands came up and latched onto her forearm.

"You're going to be my escort into the church. Don't try me. You've heard how I feel about cops. The rumors are true." She set her lips up against his ear. "I want to kill you," she whispered. "Believe me."

Aaron grabbed her crutch and used it to fend off the officers who stepped in too close. A couple of them withdrew their firearms.

"Set the gun down!" the closest one shouted.

"Not a chance," Sarah yelled back. "Shoot me, and you shoot Detective Hirst." She spun her prisoner around to face the cop who had yelled at her. "There is a sniper above us. People will die if I don't get a free pass into that church right now. Uh oh, you made me wait too long—"

What sounded like a rifle crackled from above. Someone screamed. Sarah kept her eyes on the officer aiming his gun at her, but he looked in the direction of the scream.

Aaron moved between Sarah and the cop. "See? She wasn't bluffing. One down."

"And every minute I stand here, another person will be shot."

The cop lowered his weapon. "Let her be," he shouted for the benefit of his colleagues around him. "Give her a free pass."

Sarah backed up. Then she turned toward the church and forced Hirst to start walking.

"You'll never be able to walk away from this," Hirst said.

"Shut the fuck up!" Sarah shouted in his ear.

"Canadians are *nice*. They didn't lock you up for what

you did to that cop. But down here, you'll go away for a long time for this. Kidnapping a cop and executing a civilian to make a point. Man, you're looking at a minimum of twenty years and—"

She smashed the gun into the side of his head. "When I say shut up, I'm not talking to myself. Another word out of you, and I'll shoot you in the foot. Aaron will drag you into the church. Now fuck off and keep your ramblings to yourself. I'm trying to save your life, and here I thought I could trust you."

As if Hirst was her large football and Aaron her blocker running interference ahead, the river of people spread apart, allowing them a clear path to the front doors of the church. At the steps, Sarah leaned on Hirst's shoulders to ascend them without the crutch, but she kept the gun pressed firmly against his neck. At the large wooden doors, Aaron stopped and got behind her.

The rifle crackled again.

"Shit," Sarah whispered. "I'm coming!" she yelled over her shoulder.

They entered the church. People lingered everywhere. A line led to the coffin at the front, where grieving parishioners were leaving flowers and saying a few last words. Others filled the pews. No one seemed to have noticed the gun going off outside moments before.

Parkman was talking to three uniformed officers by a small office door, gesturing wildly at different points within the church.

As Sarah glanced his way, Parkman turned to look at them, his eyes widening.

"We have a huge problem, Hirst," Sarah said. He hadn't

let go of her forearm. She hadn't dropped the gun from poking his neck yet, either. "In ten minutes, whoever is still in this church, will die."

"Bullshit. You can't know that unless you're in on it."

"Bullshit. You called me to L.A. because you know who I am and what I can do." She forced him to turn back toward the doors. "Look above the doors on the wall."

A black box the size of a small briefcase was affixed to the stone wall. A red dot blinked on the bottom of the case.

"Father Adams would always have unfettered access to this church, even when it was empty. He planted black boxes everywhere. I guess they're on a timer and set to explode at four this afternoon."

She turned to look outside. The police pushed people back farther and tightened the area they had cordoned off. No one walked the street directly in front of the church, and the rifle hadn't gone off again.

"Over here," Aaron said. He gestured at the pews beside him three rows up. "Another black case right here."

"You see, Hirst. This was the only way to get you in here. Will you help me now?"

Hirst's head swiveled from the black case to Parkman, then to Aaron.

"Aaron, relieve him of his weapon," Sarah said.

"No need," Hirst spoke fast. "I'll help. But if these aren't bombs, and you have a cell phone that talks directly to Adams, and you think this isn't about religion anymore and so on and such shit, when were you planning on letting *us* know? We're the fucking investigators."

"Ask your wife about the cell phone, and we'll talk all you want once this is over. Be cool. I'm going to release your neck. No stupid stuff because I will shoot you if I perceive you as a threat. And I won't shoot to wound. I shoot to kill. You're a cop. You understand that." His hands came away from her forearm. She lowered her arm and hopped off him. "Aaron, my crutch."

He swung it over and slipped it under her armpit. Then he stood extra close to Hirst. Aaron would stop any kind of offense Hirst had in mind. Her heart swelled at the notion.

Instead, Hirst clapped his hands loudly.

"Can I get everyone's attention?"

"Back door," Sarah said. "Adams can see the front. Get them moving out the back."

"I need everyone to leave the building as quickly as possible. This is an evacuation. We don't have time to explain. Right now, everyone has to leave the church for their own personal safety. Come on," he clapped again. "Everyone up and out. All officers, help guide the people out the back as the front is cut off now."

Some mumbled and complained, but the people began to shuffle their feet and start moving, although it was going too slow.

Sarah checked the time. 3:54 p.m.

"Six minutes to detonation. Do this faster, Hirst. You don't want anyone inside this building in five minutes."

Parkman came up beside her. "Is that what finally made him listen? A gun to the throat?"

"A girl has to do what a girl has to do to get a man to listen. Keep calm and act accordingly, Parkman. You don't want me to pull a gun on you."

"Been there, done that. Not fun."

"And here's where I redeem myself."

"You already have," he said.

"You might think so, but I don't. What happens next is redemption. For me, for how the police feel about me, you, Aaron, everything. I am involved in saving all of these people's lives. It'll mean something after this."

"Sarah, this redemption thing isn't necessary."

She checked the clock. 3:56 p.m.

Over half of the church had been cleared. The last of the people were working their way toward the back, but they were still leaving too slowly. Firing a weapon off in the church might get them moving faster, but it might also cause a stampede, and people could get hurt.

"Come on, Hirst," she shouted at him. "Faster."

Hirst yelled for everyone to keep going but to speed it up.

There was no sign of Father Adams yet. The phone remained quiet. Everyone he wanted in the church was checked off and present. All he had to do was wait for the bombs to detonate, and he was in the clear. Killing them all would muddy the investigation's waters for a very long time.

"Okay, guys, time to go. We can leave through these doors."

Aaron stepped forward, and Parkman joined him. Once they were through the double doors at the front of the church, a voice boomed behind them on a loudspeaker.

"I thank you all for coming," the metallic voice of Father Adams said. "My brother was a good man who was led astray."

Aaron and Parkman turned around and looked like they would come back inside. Balancing on one foot, Sarah grabbed both doors and pulled, slamming them shut before either man could sneak a hand inside and stop their forward motion.

Aaron yelled from the other side of the doors as something banged into them, jolting Sarah backward. Quickly, before she lost her ability to keep them out, she dropped a thick wooden bolt down, securing the two doors together. Something rammed into them again, but all they did was budge slightly. There was no way Aaron was getting back in unless Sarah allowed him to.

"Sarah, you don't have to do this!" Parkman yelled.

Sarah set her mouth to the crack between the wooden doors. "It's the only way. I'm seeking redemption. Now I've saved your life. I've saved Aaron's life. And the countless lives of the people leaving through the back, not to mention the lives of all the police officers just trying to get through each and every day. So don't fuck this up for me. Step away from the doors. You saw the bomb above them. It'll go off in about a minute. You do not want to be this close when it does. Go away, boys, and remember, I love you both."

Neither man replied. They were probably already running around to the back to try to get in.

More than fifty people still waited to exit through the rear access door.

Father Adams's voice boomed from the loudspeakers as he talked about the life of his beloved brother.

The cell phone said 3:59 p.m.

She raised the gun in her hand and fired. The remaining people ducked and looked back at her.

"Get out!" she yelled as she started toward them. "Get out now! Or I will kill you all!" She used the backs of the pews to support her weight. "Get out!" She yelled louder and raised the gun to fire into the ceiling. Father Adams' voice droned on.

Her stomach twisted, and she suddenly had the urge to throw up. Her hand missed the back of a pew, and she fell, hitting the church's floor, pain shooting through her abdomen. She clenched her teeth and scrunched her eyes closed.

"Shit, that hurt."

A tickling on the nape of her neck and a whisper in her ear from Vivian reminded her that if she didn't get up and keep moving, something was about to happen that would hurt a whole lot more.

Sometimes, there are more important things than a cracked ribcage and a broken foot.

She rolled to her knees, screamed as her ribs were on fire, grabbed the side of a pew, and forced herself to her feet, her head spinning at the pain.

Father Adams's voice continued as if the entire church was full of listeners held rapt at the life of a religious man. She used his obnoxious voice to motivate her to move to the next pew. Then the next.

After three, she checked the time.

4:00 p.m.

Any second, the entire church would explode. She wouldn't make it. Going in, she knew there wasn't a good chance of her walking out of this, but there was no other choice. Fortunate enough to be the one privy to the inside information, she was the only one who could get the building evacuated in time. That meant staying with the ship as it went down.

But maybe the bombs were on a different clock. Maybe

their timers were a minute or two slower than the cell phone's.

Five more pews, and she'd be at the front of the church. The people at the back door were filing out. Three, two, one, and then Hirst turned to look at her. Their eyes met. She waved him off.

"Lock the door," she shouted over Father Adams's voice. "Get everyone as far away from the building as possible."

Hirst nodded.

"Oh, and Hirst. Thanks."

The door slammed shut. She was alone with Adams's voice booming through the loudspeakers. She had done it. She had emptied the church. Now it was time for the last act.

Her energy waning, and the crutch back near the front of the church, Sarah hopped on her right leg as she crossed the open space heading to the large crucifix by the baptismal font.

Something clicked behind her.

She didn't look back. Three hops left.

Another click.

Two hops.

When the first bomb exploded, the interior pressure was contained for the briefest of moments, then it expanded into an intense shock wave. One second, Sarah was hopping on a leg she wasn't sure would hold her up, and the next, she was airborne as the concussion hit her from behind.

Without knowing how she understood, the devices were exploding one after another. Even as her short flight ended and she smacked down, the second one blew and then the third.

A rolling wall of flames followed the shock waves of

each incendiary device.

She closed her eyes as her eyebrows and lashes singed off. The bombs continued to explode throughout the centuries-old church, silencing Father Adams's metallic voice.

It also silenced everything else for Sarah Roberts.

Chapter 36

Parkman, with Aaron following close behind, had gotten around back and was running for the door as Detective Hirst walked away from it.

"Hirst!" Parkman yelled. "Where's Sarah? Did she come out this way?"

Hirst shook his head in the negative.

"We have to get in there," Parkman said, frantic with the thought that Sarah would die.

Hirst stepped in his way. "Parkman, if she wanted out, she had her chance."

"No. She. Didn't." Parkman fought to get past Hirst.

Aaron ran around them. Hirst lunged out, but he was too slow and missed.

A loud explosion ruptured the air. The ground shook under their feet. Then Parkman scrambled toward the door.

Another explosion followed the first. Then another. The

windows in the back of the church blew out, raining stained glass down on Aaron and Parkman.

Feeling every bit the coward, Parkman turned and ran from the church as more explosions rocked its foundation. Aaron stayed on his heels.

The church soon dissolved into four walls and rubble with charred skeletal remains. The buildings across the street in the front and back had all their windows blown out, too.

Parkman got knocked to the ground with the last couple of explosions, igniting the pain from the bullet wound. With all the walking around, running, and now smashing into the ground, he was sure he had reopened the stitches. But it was nothing to what Sarah was going through. She was still inside the church.

"Sarah!" Aaron shouted beside him. "*Sarah!*"

Tears streaked down his face as he attempted to approach the church but was pushed back by the intensity of the heat.

Parkman lay flat out on the concrete, his head raised to watch as the flames engulfed what was once a magnificent church.

There was no getting out of that building alive. All four walls took a hit as the man behind the destruction had planned carefully, placing his explosives strategically. If Sarah were still in that building, it would be virtually impossible for her to still be alive.

Parkman blinked up at the L.A. sky. As the fire trucks arrived, he cried.

It was his fault they were here in the first place. None of this would've happened had he not agreed to bring Sarah. What was he thinking? She had a broken foot. She almost died on the fifth floor of that parking garage. She could've been run over by Father Adams's brother when Officer Vicky Chard got hit by that white van. And what about the pimp who pulled a gun on her? Sarah dodged death like Wonder Woman dodged bullets. But now she had gone one too far.

He wiped at his eyes.

One too far.

"I'm so sorry, Sarah."

"Don't say that!" Aaron yelled. "She'll make it. She has to. It's Sarah we're talking about here."

A loud crashing sound and a corresponding ground-shaking boom followed a huge bang.

What the fuck was that?

Hirst stepped close to Aaron. "I'm sorry, guys. No one is walking out of that church alive."

Parkman lifted his head to see what made the terrible noise. The roof of the church had collapsed. Flames raced toward the sky from all over the church, the stone walls already blackening at the top. Flames rushed out the broken windows in the back as if eager to breathe fresh air.

A long stream of water from a fire truck soared above the ruined remains and landed in a misty spray as it came in contact with the flames. Another stream followed the first. Then another.

Too late. Too damn late.

Parkman wept at the loss of Sarah Roberts.

Aaron fell to his knees beside Parkman. After a moment, grief overtook him, and he pressed his forehead against the ground and cried, whispering "No" over and over.

Parkman wondered if he would burn in Hell for bringing Sarah to L.A. How would God look at him when he died one day after sacrificing his star player down here? She was the one girl that could save and help people.

"I'm so sorry, Sarah. Please forgive me."

He rolled onto his side and cried violently for the loss of his friend, his confidante.

He was still there when fire trucks came up the back road to work on the flames from this side.

Two firemen had to help him to an ambulance. They wanted to see why he was bleeding.

His stitches had ripped open. But that didn't matter. Nothing mattered now. Nothing mattered anymore.

He looked back at what was left of the church.

Sarah Roberts was dead.

Chapter 37

HER LEG WAS EXHAUSTED on her last hop, but she was still too far away. The first explosion hit her from behind, knocking her off her foot. She landed in the center of the baptismal font. The circular marble fountain was over eight feet in diameter. The explosion gave her the extra boost needed, as her final hop would've fallen short.

A burning heat covered her body the instant she was airborne, then cooled just as instantly when submerged in the water of the font. She dropped to the bottom of the water and secured her hands to the sides to remain as low as possible.

Explosion after explosion rippled above her. Flames roared over the font like an angry orange cloud, held back by the cover of water in its attempt to touch her. But her time in the baptismal font was coming to an end.

More explosions sounded throughout the church. It was falling apart, leaving her exposed. Another explosion blew chunks of rock and stone over the font, small pieces landing in the water.

She needed to breathe. Her lungs were starving, but the air above the font had blackened, the only light coming from the intense flames already consuming the church.

The marble cracked beside her head. Water began to gush out of the ruined font. Her legs, which had floated higher than her upper body, were exposed to the heat-charged air in seconds.

She dropped to her knees, kept her head low, and as the water emptied, she cupped her hands over her nose and breathed in three times rapidly. Then she dove over the side, hoping she wouldn't knock herself unconscious with the pain in her ribs.

She landed hard, rolled onto a burning piece of wood, and rolled off it just as fast. Her yelp brought an influx of raw, blackened air into her lungs. She coughed and hacked, her eyes blurring, her rib cage causing its own fire.

As her lungs struggled to cope with limited oxygen, her wet clothes and hair offered a shield from the flames and heat. She had a minute, maybe less, before her smoking clothes would lose their moisture, then catch fire.

Sarah got onto her hands and knees, kept her head low, and crawled as fast as she could toward the side of the building. A deafening crash obliterated her hearing momentarily. She looked over her shoulder long enough to see a part of the wooden roof had collapsed, destroying what was left of the baptismal font she had just vacated.

After another coughing bout, she pushed on, her head getting foggy.

Vivian, where are you when I need you most?

Her arms gave way, and she dropped to her elbows. Another crash behind her shook the floor. The thought of a thousand-pound chunk of a stone wall or a large piece of the wooden roof crushing her like a watermelon forced her to push on using her elbows instead of hands, her nose skimming the ground in search of any remaining oxygen.

The wet clothes had become lighter, now only a thin dampness against her skin. It was like the sun was crashing into the Earth, and her crawling away was as pointless as an ant rushing along the sidewalk before a large shoe came down.

The last breath she inhaled tasted like dead air, soot, and thick dust, offering no oxygen for the muscles she needed to use. She coughed hard to clear her lungs, then cupped her hands over her mouth and nose to breathe as her eyes watered with the effort.

More crashing behind her. Something else smashed down. One quick look over her shoulder showed the blue sky through the towering flames.

Directly above her was a stone outcropping where the second-floor stone balcony started.

The coughing and hacking caused her vision to dim. Collapsing now meant death. The fire behind her crept closer as all the wooden pews roared in flames. Other things fell and smashed to the floor. The crazy sound of police sirens and fire trucks reached her deep inside the church.

She pushed on again, her clothes no longer wet, clinging to her as if she wore them to a sauna. Her arms weakened and gave way, and her chin connected with the stone floor. But now her head had dipped lower than her body. She faltered. Her consciousness wavered, threatening to succumb to the elements around her.

Why is my neck craned downward? Is there a hole in the floor?

Her oxygen-starved mind lost focus. One of Vivian's foreign thoughts entered her consciousness, crisp and clear.

Stairs.

The stairs to the crypt.

The fire raged closer. Something banged somewhere in the church. More sirens reached her.

As Sarah coughed, pain wracked her chest, waking her enough to open her eyes again. She blinked rapidly to see through the black smoke. An opening, dark and cool, lay before her. The darkness of the church's crypt beckoned her.

With the last bit of energy, she pushed with her foot as she pulled on the edge of the stairs. Then she did it again. She wondered if a lung could collapse under these conditions.

By the third stair, her body weight and momentum eased her down headfirst. She slid along the fieldstone steps as if she were a sled made of jelly. The air was cleaner. It was sweet and cool and tasted delicious. The heat dissipated instantly at the bottom of the steps, the cool air gently touching her heat-ravaged skin.

At the bottom, she rolled onto her back and coughed to clear her lungs, but it didn't work. It felt like a layer of black soot coated them on the inside.

Debris from above followed her down a few steps. She had to get deeper. A corner somewhere, an alcove.

The crypt's roof was made of stone. It left her with the impression that it was excavated before the church was built, and the designers fortified the crypt to withstand earthquakes.

She couldn't crawl anymore, and the pain in her chest

was too intense to keep using her arms. The coughing aggravated the cracked rib, and her skin ached all over her body from the heat above.

Slightly more alert with the cooler, cleaner air of the crypt, Sarah tucked her arms to her side and rolled. She rolled in the darkness, waiting for a wall or an abutment to cease her spinning.

There must've been a downward slope in the crypt because she was suddenly rolling faster than expected. She coughed, shouted at the pain, instinctively curled into a ball, and slammed against a stone wall, her broken foot hitting the wall first.

The pain from her wounds raised a fire on the inside. It was the last cough, the last scream, that gagged her. She hacked, thinking she would vomit as her throat constricted, choking on her gag reflex.

Then, fortunately, she passed out, and the pain was no more.

Temporarily.

Chapter 38

PARKMAN WAS HELPED BACK to an ambulance, where paramedics tried to get him inside the vehicle.

"But sir, we need to redress that wound."

"Do it out here," Parkman said. "I can't have the church out of my sight. I'm not going to any hospital."

The paramedics stepped away and conferred out of earshot as Aaron walked over, his face a mask of dirt. Tears had cleared paths down his cheeks. The fire raged behind him, and the stone walls blackened.

"You okay?" Aaron asked.

"Not really."

"What's up with these two?" Aaron gestured at the paramedics. "It looked like they were arguing with you."

"They want to redress my wound."

"Sounds like a good idea. What's the issue?"

Parkman met Aaron's eyes. "The redressing won't take

place here, and I am not going to the local hospital. I won't leave this area until the flames are out and we've either found her body or discovered her alive."

Aaron's eyes watered. "Parkman, there's a reality we may have to face here, but I don't give up easy."

"Neither do I."

"When she locked that door, and we ran around to the back, she didn't come out. According to Hirst, she was still by the pews in the center of the church, firing her weapon into the ceiling and yelling about how everyone else had to get out. There was no way she made it. The roof caved in within minutes from the first explosion." He wiped at more tears. "We must face the fact that she sacrificed herself for us and all those people."

"And the cops that lined both sides of those pews," Parkman added, a hint of anger in his voice. "After all they did for Sarah in her short life, let's not forget the sacrifice she made for those cops."

"I guess she got her wish."

"What wish was that?" Parkman asked.

"To be redeemed."

"That was one of the last things she said. But if cleaning the slate for her meant death, then she's a twisted girl because I'd rather her be alive and angry at me than dead."

"Be careful what you wish for. Sarah angry at you isn't a pretty thought."

The attempt at humor didn't go over well. They both looked at the church as the Los Angeles Fire Department battled the flames that had a life of their own as if fueled by Hell itself.

"You two okay?" Hirst walked up to them. He saw the

fresh blood on Parkman. "Hey guys," he said to the paramedics, still talking on the side. "You gonna do something about that?"

"He won't let us take him to the hospital."

Hirst turned to Parkman. "Why not? There's no way anyone will be walking through that church until morning. Go get stitched up, rest for the evening, and come back. I'll authorize a personal walkthrough of the crime scene as soon as it's deemed safe."

One of the paramedics stepped in front of Parkman with a piece of paper and a pen.

"Excuse me, sir. If you won't come to the hospital and let us do our job, I must ask you to sign this form acknowledging that you denied our help."

Parkman pushed the paper aside. "Don't worry about it. I'll go with you. But on one condition."

"What's that, sir?"

Parkman turned to Aaron. "Any news on Sarah is called into me first."

Aaron nodded. "Of course."

Parkman allowed the paramedics to lift him inside the ambulance. Moments later, they pulled away.

Parkman whispered a prayer for Sarah as he wept all the way to the hospital.

Chapter 39

Aaron later joined Parkman at the hospital, where they were offered two beds in their own room for the night. Sleep had been elusive. The last time Aaron checked the clock, it had been after three in the morning.

He snapped awake. 7:34 a.m.

No one had called his cell.

He jumped out of bed, used the bathroom, and stepped into the hall to call Hirst. "Anything new?"

"Nothing. Fire marshals and investigators are about to begin their walkthrough of the burned-out remains, but that's it."

"She didn't turn up anywhere, hand waving in the air, shouting something like, 'I'm okay'?"

"No." There was a pause. "I'm sorry."

"I'll rouse Parkman. We'll come down."

"Okay. And I've got something I want you two to look

at."

"What?"

"Sarah said something before she forced me into the church."

"What'd she say?"

"When you get here. Nothing will change between now and then."

"Okay."

Half an hour later, Parkman and Aaron were in a taxi on their way to the remains of the church. They rode in silence.

The fire department had blocked the area around the burned-out building. Aaron got the driver to maneuver as close as he could. Hirst started toward them.

The blackened skeletal remains of support beams were all that was left of Sarah's grave. Where sections of the stone walls still stood, he saw her strength in life. And where the roof was gone, leaving only ashes in its wake, he envisioned his heart, in ashes, burned and empty after having known and loved Sarah.

"Why?" he mumbled under his breath, her loss not completely registering yet.

"Why?" Parkman nodded beside him, looking like he came off the set of *The Walking Dead*.

The taxi pulled away as Hirst walked up.

"What did you want to tell us?" Aaron asked Hirst.

"It's about what Sarah said before she entered the church."

"What did she say?"

"That she didn't believe this was about Catholicism."

"What could she mean by that? What'd she think this was about?"

"She didn't say exactly."

"And?" Aaron frowned. "What have you learned? Found any bodies? Uncovered some random truth?"

"Aaron," Parkman said softly. "Easy. This wasn't his fault."

"I know." Aaron looked at the ground. "I'm just angry."

"Understandably." Hirst patted Aaron's shoulder. "Across the street in that building," Hirst pointed, "there's an empty apartment on the third floor. The sniper was set up in there. We found bullet casings, an empty coffee cup, and the gun he used."

"Was there a name on the lease?" Aaron asked. "Who was it rented to?"

"A man named Mike, last name Myers, like the actor. But we think it's Michael, as in Father Michael Adams."

"Wasn't Mike Myers the name of the killer in the movie Halloween?"

Parkman asked, "Any physical trace of him there? Anything that'll lead us to where he might be?"

"They're dusting for prints. We only found the apartment two hours ago. What we've got so far is he used a microphone from across the street to blast his voice inside the church. He fired on us and watched as the church blew up."

"Which means he wasn't in the church. He escaped."

Hirst nodded. "That's right. But we'll catch up with him sooner or later."

"Or I will," Aaron said in a matter-of-fact tone.

"No, we don't need a male version of Sarah running around L.A."

"What else do you have?" Parkman asked. "Or can we walk through the ruins now?"

"We've got tax records, deeds, and everything else we could find with Father Adams's name on it." Hirst grinned. It was the first time Aaron had seen the man grin like that. "Guess what we found."

"No time," Aaron said, the idea of humor lost on him. "Just tell us."

"According to tax records, Father Adams and his brother have been writing off building materials to the tune of a million dollars each."

"Building materials? For what? A new church?"

Hirst shook his head in an exaggerated way. "No. We think they're building a new luxury home somewhere to go with the Rolls Royce he bought last year."

"Rolls Royce? Don't they go for a couple of hundred grand or something?"

"At least."

"On a priest's salary?" Aaron said. "Shit, I might have found a new calling."

Hirst was shaking his head again. "He doesn't make that much."

"So what's Adams been up to? Embezzling from the church?"

"Bingo." Hirst smacked a fist into his palm. "Over the past year, Father Adams had been under internal investigation for theft from the church. And guess which four churches under Father Adams had declared money missing?"

"The same four that recently had a priest killed," Parkman said. "He was silencing his opposition like he tried to do with us."

"Bingo again."

"So where are all these building supplies?" Aaron asked.

"What was he building?"

"We don't know yet. We're working on it."

A man in a suit jacket wearing a fireman's badge stepped up to Hirst. "You guys can walk through now. Just be careful, and we're not responsible for injuries. Not everything is cleared out yet, but it'll take days to get started."

"Any bodies yet?" Aaron asked.

The man shook his head. "None."

"Then there's still hope."

"Come on, I'll escort you around."

Aaron grabbed Parkman's arm. "Let's go say goodbye. Then find Adams and punch his ticket to Hell."

Chapter 40

Inside the church, nothing resembled the beauty it once was. Various sections of the four walls still stood, but that was it. The wooden pews were gone, replaced by a blackened floor with random mounds of burned debris. The large crucifix near the front was gone. Chunks of stone from the walls lay scattered about.

"The floor seems to have held up," the fire investigator said as he walked them toward the center. "This one was modeled after Italian Catholic churches. We had the city send over the plans before we started trampling around."

Aaron tried to imagine where he was when he stepped outside yesterday. Where had Sarah been? When she locked them out, where could she have gone? He turned and surveyed the wall to where the back door had been. Somewhere between these two spots was where they would find Sarah's remains. Slowed by a broken foot, there was no way she could be anywhere else.

Parkman and the investigator had walked ahead. Aaron turned and followed, a glumness falling over him. What was life all about if you loved and lived and then the best ones were taken away from you? If life was about lessons, then what the hell was death about?

Sarah was needed. Sarah had a purpose. She was helping humanity and had almost died several times. Why now? And why didn't Vivian step in?

Aaron looked skyward and raised a fist.

"This is on you, Vivian."

The blue sky above him didn't respond. It was Parkman's voice that made him jump.

"Over here!" Parkman called from beside a pile of soot-covered junk.

"What'd you find?" Aaron called back.

"Help move this shit out of the way."

"Parkman, what are you doing?"

Aaron started over to see what had riled up Parkman. Other investigators took notice and headed Parkman's way, too.

When Aaron got to Parkman's side, Hirst was moving a large stone out of the way.

"What's going on, guys?" Aaron asked.

"Stairs," Parkman said.

"To what?"

"The crypt."

Those two words were like a punch in the stomach. Of course. The crypt. Sarah had a lot of experience with crypts from her time in Italy years ago when she was hunting Armond Stuart, a human trafficker. Aaron had also heard the stories about Esztergom and the crypts in Hungary.

Before getting his hopes up, he looked at how far the crypt's opening was from where Sarah would have likely been when the explosions started. She might have made it to the crypt with two good feet and a running chance, but probably not, especially not with a broken foot.

"She couldn't have made it this far, Parkman. I don't want to be a naysayer, but by the time she locked the front door, there was no way she had the time to run down into the crypt."

The fire investigator looked forlorn at Aaron as if to say that he felt bad for the false hope Parkman exuded. "Yeah," he said. "Consider the intensity of the fire, too. That kind of fire needs a ton of oxygen. Any oxygen down in the crypt would've been sucked up and used. It would've made breathing hard, not to mention the water from the fire trucks. That would've collected down there. In this kind of fire, if it weren't the smoke or the fire, the water would drown you."

Parkman tossed a charred piece of wood aside and stopped to examine the fire investigator.

"Sarah's a survivor. She's immortal, like a fucking vampire. She would if she could find a way to survive down there among the dead. I don't want to be the one to tell her that she has to stay trapped a little longer because no one believed she could do it. My guess is she will be seriously pissed when we get to her, and she will want a glass of whiskey and a bed. So, will you help me clear these stairs, or will we keep debating her tenacity?"

The investigator grabbed a piece of stone and tossed it aside. He worked without looking at Parkman or responding to his last question.

Aaron got in on it and worked beside Parkman, who was doing very little because of his injuries. Hirst and a few fire guys began organizing the debris in piles, keeping it away from the crypt's opening as the three men reached the bottom of the stairs.

"Anyone got a flashlight?" Parkman asked. "We're almost through."

A long black mag light was handed down to him. Aaron and the investigator heaved a large piece of wall aside, and Parkman stepped into the clearing. Then Aaron jumped down to join him.

"Over here," Aaron said. "Shine the light this way."

They walked the interior of the crypt until they got to an area where the ground sloped downward. The floor's stones were damp from the fire hoses. Moving slowly in a grid formation, they scoured the crypt's cavernous area.

Drainage grates were built into the floor in case of flooding. Two of them had standing water at their edges.

That's why the water isn't thigh-high down here.

Aaron was losing any hope Parkman might have instilled as each section of the crypt and corner was empty.

"In that corner at the back. More debris."

As he said it, he realized debris wouldn't have come this far inside the crypt.

Parkman swung the flashlight in Aaron's direction, and they both gasped.

Sarah lay sprawled on the stone floor, her body a mask of black and red. Her clothes were burnt in spots. Her long hair had been singed in places. Under the flashlight's glow, Aaron was close enough to see her eyebrows were missing.

"Sarah," he gasped, his voice caught in his throat as he

ran over and dropped to his knees. He touched her neck for a pulse, then shuddered and made a guttural sound.

Parkman set the flashlight down, keeping it aimed at Sarah, and scurried away. On the other side of the cavernous room, Parkman shouted up for an ambulance.

"We've got a survivor down here!" he yelled.

The words coming from Parkman were so sweet for Aaron to hear, he could almost taste them.

Sarah's pulse was solid. She was alive. She was asleep, no doubt completely exhausted.

But how did she do it? How could she pull this off?

"That's impossible," the investigator yelled back. "Is this a joke?"

"I'm going to fucking kill you if I have to come up there," Parkman yelled back. "Get me paramedics and oxygen down here yesterday." He paused. "Hirst?"

"Yeah?"

"Sarah's alive."

Aaron could barely hear what Hirst said, but it sounded like a bewildered, "Holy shit."

"I know. But we need help."

"I'm on it. We'll have help down to you in minutes."

Sarah stirred under Aaron's hand.

"Baby, you're okay now," he whispered.

She coughed.

Aaron teared up. He couldn't believe it.

She coughed harder, then winced in pain.

He rubbed her back as she tried unsuccessfully to get her lungs under control.

"Oxygen!" Parkman yelled from the base of the stairs. "Now!" he yelled louder. "Toss me a tank."

"You're okay, Sarah." Aaron touched her forehead. "You're going to make it."

Under the flashlight's glow, Sarah tried to open her eyes but failed.

"Aaron?" Her voice was raspy.

"Right here, baby."

"Did we catch … the bastard?"

"Not yet."

She coughed. "I need a vacation."

"Agreed. Time for a break."

"Hurry the fuck up!" Parkman yelled again.

"Parkman?" Sarah asked.

"Yeah, baby, he's getting oxygen for you."

"Yeah … could use some of that." She offered a half smile.

"Just rest. Don't talk. Breathe slowly. It's coming."

"Don't tell me what—" she coughed.

"No, I said don't talk."

"Don't tell me what to do. I'm not dead yet."

"We're going to get you out of here."

"Promise me something—" A wracking cough cut her off.

When she quieted and breathed slowly, Aaron asked, "What's that?"

"I'm the one who goes after the priest. He's mine. Those bombs were not a girl's idea of an explosive night out."

"No problem, baby. No problem. But first, vacation."

"No vacation. After. First, kill the priest."

"Yes, dear. Got it. Kill the priest."

"I don't appreciate being inside a building when it goes up in flames."

"Can't argue with that."

"Good." She coughed, then breathed deeply as if the air was being siphoned through a tube. It sounded like her throat was constricting, and it bothered Aaron to hear it. "Because it's an argument you'd lose."

"Still the same old Sarah. But now you sound like the Godfather, all raspy and shit."

"You bet your ass. Now get me out of here. I got a man of God to send to Hell."

"I thought you didn't believe in Hell."

"I do now."

Parkman was on his way back, an oxygen tank in his hand.

"What changed your mind?"

"I've seen it. Inside God's house. Inside this church. And it isn't pretty."

"Whoever said Hell was pretty?"

"Stop with the asinine questions and silly humor." She smiled. "Just get me out of here."

"With pleasure."

Chapter 41

*W*HY AM *I* ALWAYS *in hospitals?*

A subtle discomfort simmered in her lungs like she'd inhaled chili pepper, but it had gotten better. Minus a little hair and a couple of burn marks on her skin, she would be fine.

"How did you manage to get to the crypt without getting burned or blown apart?" Hirst asked.

"When the first bomb hit, I landed in the baptismal font. The water protected me, and the marble exterior insulated me. Until it cracked."

"Then what?" Aaron asked.

"I got out, kept low, and crawled for the crypt, soaking wet. I remember faltering at the top of the stairs like I would pass out. But part of the roof crashed down, snapping me out of it. I made it down the stairs and rolled into the far corner of the crypt."

"You passed out with your mouth and nose directly over the farthest grate," Hirst added. "When oxygen was pulled up to fuel the fire, the grates kept a constant flow of air passing by your face. As the crypt filled with water, all the drainage grates at the front of the crypt kept most of the water away from you."

Parkman shook his head. "No one else could've survived that. Incredible."

The room was inundated with cards and flowers. It was like everybody in Los Angeles thought she was some kind of second coming. The media had picked up the miraculous survival of Sarah Roberts. And not just her survival but how she got everyone out beforehand.

"All these cards," Hirst said, "came from officers and their families, and the other hundred we haven't opened came from people in the church. You have a lot of people out there wanting to thank you."

"Too bad Vivian doesn't get the thanks. It was all her doing."

Hirst smiled. "Sarah, you stepped up. When I didn't listen to you, you put a gun to my neck and made me listen. Nobody has ever done that to me and then gotten a thank you after. You have saved so many lives, cops' lives, our lives, that every cop in the country—scratch that—continent wants to shake your hand."

"Have I altered my image, my public relations persona? Fixed the preconceived idea of who Sarah Roberts is?"

"Absolutely. As far as I can tell."

"Good, because there's an ex-cop that I need to find soon."

"Who are you talking about?" Aaron asked.

"A cop I knew when I was eight or nine years old. But I don't think he's a cop anymore."

"I can help you with that," Hirst said. "It's the least I can do."

"Thanks, but I have to do this one on my own." She cleared her throat, coughed, and cleared it again. "Any chance you can bring me up to speed on what you've got on Adams?"

Hirst shook his head. "Nope. Sorry. You're out for sure now. The fight for you is over. As a civilian, I could never authorize you to come back into the fold after what happened. You're out, Sarah."

"I'm out when Adams is out."

Hirst snapped his head back in surprise. "Parkman, can you tell her?"

"Nope. Sorry. She doesn't listen to me."

"Then who does she listen to?" Hirst asked.

"Vivian and my intuition," Sarah said. "That's it."

"You've got a broken foot. You were shot and wrapped up by a hungry python for dinner. You had to kill it by slamming your rental car into the concrete from the top of a five-story parking garage. Then you walked away from an explosion that leveled a church, and you want to return when you're getting a free pass to leave, go home, and sleep for a century?"

"That's why I love her," Aaron said. "Only death will stop this one. And even then, I wouldn't be so sure. Her sister lingers after death. I wonder what Sarah would be like ..."

"Aaron, if you don't stop talking about death, I might have to cause one."

"Got it."

They smiled at each other. She winked at him, then turned her attention back to Hirst. Since she met Hirst, he'd aged some. Or maybe she hadn't looked close enough. Lines formed around his eyes when he smiled. A streak of gray colored his hair on each side just above the ears. The sclera of his eyes had darkened with blood, and his tie was undone. The stress over the past couple of weeks had taken a toll, but Sarah knew the only way to stop Father Adams was to involve her.

"Detective Hirst, I'm here to help. I know I'm physically out, but I can still help. I promise when Father Adams is dealt with, I will leave L.A. But until then, I believe I can still help. Tell me about Adams's finances. What have you discovered?"

Hirst looked at Parkman, then back at Sarah. "Did he tell you?"

"No. But I suspect you found something. I don't believe this was as religion based as I previously thought."

Hirst took a seat beside Parkman at a small table in the corner of Sarah's room. Aaron stayed on the chair beside her bed, holding her hand.

"I'll tell you because you deserve that much. But you're still out."

"You think I can do anything with this?" She gestured along her body. "Now, what have you got?"

"Large amounts of money have disappeared from a few of the local churches. The dead priests had been working together to expose Father Adams, but they were probably all afraid to step forward without absolute proof. Each of those priests had been suspected of crimes in the past, and Father Adams was tasked to cover it up. The church deals with these things internally. Saying anything against Father Adams might have exposed them as well. Perhaps speaking out would cause Father Adams to be replaced, and they'd have to deal with someone else. Someone they didn't know."

"Speculation after speculation," Parkman said.

"But what have you discovered about Father Adams personally?" Sarah asked.

"Building materials were billed to the church."

"For what? To build what?"

Hirst steepled his hands. "With all the computers today, the research available to us, and the financial accountability of such an organization, we can't find a single reference to a location. Simply put, we have no idea what Adams was building or where. We don't know what he was up to or why. Father Adams has disappeared, and we have nothing but the aftermath to deal with. He bought a Rolls Royce, but that's the only solid lead to where the money's gone."

"I think I know," Sarah said, her voice a bit raspy. She took a sip of water from the glass beside her. "I think I know where he is."

"Where?" Parkman asked.

All three men stared at her.

"He didn't succeed in his plan to kill us in his church at his brother's eulogy. He really wanted me, but he would take the rest of you if he could."

"Gee, thanks," Aaron said.

"Yeah, great." Parkman popped a toothpick in his mouth. "I like being an afterthought when it comes to my own murder."

"You guys done?" Sarah asked, not able to hide her smile.

They nodded.

"He's planning another hit."

"He hasn't had enough?" Hirst asked.

"He believes we've been lucky. He believes his mission is *ordained*."

"By God? How could he think that after all the killing he's done?"

"Not by God."

"Then by whom?"

His eyes widened when it donned on Hirst, and he loosened his tie. "Son of a bitch. The guy's off his rocker."

"Which is all the more reason we must deal with him."

Sarah took in the clean, wonderful air in the silence that followed. After crawling into that crypt, the hospital air tasted so rich.

"Can't you just get your sister to let you know where Father Adams is right now?" Hirst asked.

"I already know where he is."

"Why haven't you told us?" Hirst snapped.

"Because where he is isn't as important as where he'll be."

"What does that mean? Then where will he be?"

"I know where he'll be in thirty minutes."

"What?" Hirst nearly shouted. He snapped a look at Parkman, who shrugged.

"Don't look at me," Parkman said. "It's always better when Sarah's in charge. Just listen to what she has to say. Then do what she tells you to do. It minimizes casualties."

"Okay, where will he be, and what do you want me to do?"

"I want your gun for protection."

"No way. It's a police-registered weapon. I cannot give you this gun. I'll get you another one. When do you need it by?"

"There's no time for another gun. I need yours."

"Why mine?" Hirst asked. "I'm at a loss here. What's going on?"

"I need yours so you can take the credit for the kill after he's dead. You'll be the hero L.A. needs."

"What are you talking about?"

"Trust."

He sat back in his chair and rubbed his chin. Clearly, in a spot he never wanted to be in, Hirst had a decision to make, and Sarah wouldn't let him think about it too long.

"Don't overthink this. You'll head fuck it if you do. Just go with it. Just do what I say, and I will deliver Father Adams's body to you. It's the only way. You have to trust me."

Hirst stared at her without responding.

"If I'm wrong, and it all turns out bad, just say I overpowered you and stole your weapon."

"Yeah, that'll work just fine. Overpowered by a girl in your condition."

"Watch it," Aaron said. "She's still got a lot of fight left in her."

"It's okay." Sarah touched Aaron's arm. "Tell them I had Aaron take the weapon. That would work. Whoever knows us would understand."

Hirst unclipped his holster and pulled his weapon out, holding it with two fingers. "For the record, I don't agree with this, but I have no choice but to trust you. Where do you want it?"

"Taped to the bottom of my IV stand."

"What? How will you reach it?"

"We've got less than half an hour before I see Father Adams. Unnecessary questions will slow us down."

"He's coming here?" Parkman asked, standing from his chair.

Hirst stood too.

"Yes, he's coming here. Aaron, take the gun from Hirst and get tape. Then strap it to the bottom of the IV stand. We're running out of time."

"But if he comes here," Hirst said. "We'll nab him. Just tell me when and where."

"You can't just nab him because this time, the bombs aren't in the building. He's wearing them."

"Oh shit."

"Exactly."

Chapter 42

"Guys," Sarah said. "We've got less than ten minutes. Is everyone ready? Remember what I told you. Let him take me. Stay hidden. Don't fuck this up, or I'll be dead, and you don't want a pissed-off Sarah coming back from the other side. I won't be nice and playful like my sister."

All three men nodded in unison.

"Okay, this will hurt, but I need Aaron and Parkman to help me into that wheelchair. Detective Hirst, for this to work, you need to leave. Did you bring your cruiser or personal vehicle?"

"Cruiser. It's in visitor's parking."

"Good. Go to it. Call for backup. Tell them whatever you must, but get a couple of units here. Then come back into the hospital and bring a couple of doctors to the side door on the east side of the building." Sarah closed her eyes and rubbed her temples. "It's hard to remember everything. I'm pretty sure it's the east wing." She opened her eyes. "Yeah, east wing."

The mood in the room had turned to one of uncertainty. The men shuffled their feet. Hirst looked from Parkman to Sarah. She knew he trusted Parkman and wanted to do right by him, but Hirst struggled with taking orders from her. His job and career were on the line, not just his life.

"What's going on here?" Sarah asked. "Is there a problem?"

Aaron and Parkman looked at Hirst, knowing the question wasn't directed at them.

Hirst headed for the door. "There's no problem, Sarah. I'll do what you ask. I just hope you're right."

"I am. But there's one more thing I need you to do. Actually, it's something I need you to remember."

Hirst opened the door, looked into the corridor, and turned back. "What's that?"

"Between now and when we meet again, I want you to think about Janice."

"Janice? My wife? Why's that? How does she come into this?"

"Just do it. When the moment is right, think about Janice. You'll understand when it comes to you."

Hirst nodded and backed out of the room.

"Okay, guys, wheel me out to the elevators. Let's go get us a priest."

Aaron stepped in front of Sarah and knelt down. "Can you tell us anything more to prepare us for what we're walking into?"

"No. Hell, I'm not prepared for this. Just roll this damn thing and think on your feet. Do that, and you'll live."

He stood up. "Think on your feet. Hmmph. I guess I can do that. How about you, Parkman? Can you think on your feet?"

"Are you asking me if I'm okay with whatever Sarah's doing here?" Parkman said.

Aaron nodded. "The guy's insane. According to Sarah, he's strapped with explosives and on his way here. All we've got is a gun taped to the bottom of this IV stand, and Sarah, who," he looked down at her, "sorry, no offense, is in no condition to fight."

"Aaron, whatever Sarah says is the way we do it. She knows if things go south, she'll have to own it. And she will. Sarah's got the advantage of listening to the other side. In my opinion, it's Sarah's way or walk away. If it doesn't fly, we all die."

"Cute. Nice rhyme." He looked back at Sarah. "I guess I just hate being a part of it when you're also going into action."

"It never gets any better, Aaron. One day you'll have to fully accept what I do."

"I do. That's why we've lasted so long."

"Then what's this? Why stop us at such a crucial moment?"

"Crawl back into that bed and rest. Let us handle this. If Father Adams is here, then we'll deal with him."

"Not going to happen. It's me he wants. I have to be the one. If you don't want to help, step aside. Parkman, push this damn wheelchair. Let's go."

They waited another heartbeat. Then Aaron got behind the chair and pushed her to the door. Parkman opened the door and peered outside the room to ensure the way was clear.

Sarah knew both men so well. Parkman had to stand back and let Aaron work through his insecurities toward the violent life Sarah willingly walked into. Aaron had to own his decision or walk away, and neither Sarah nor Parkman would ever mother him on that. He had to man up, make the choice and keep on making it until he knew, deep within himself, how his relationship with Sarah would always be.

She wanted to marry this man one day, and she couldn't have him always running after her trying to protect her. That just wouldn't do.

Aaron turned the chair to the left in the corridor and started down the hall. They waited by the elevators, adrenaline pumping through Sarah's body, minimizing some of her minor aches.

When the doors opened, Aaron pulled Sarah back to let a nurse wheel an empty gurney off, then they got on.

Moments later, on the main floor, Aaron turned her to the right, Parkman walking beside her, pushing the IV stand.

"Stop," Sarah said.

They stopped, and Parkman stepped forward, scanning the people in the corridor.

"What is it?" he asked.

"We're going the wrong way."

"No, we're not," he said. "That's the east side of the building."

"Turn me around. Go to the west side."

Aaron approached the front of the chair and exchanged a look with Parkman. "Sarah, you told Hirst to go to the east side. What gives?"

"I know what I said. But as you recall, I also said it was

pretty hard to remember everything. I said I was *pretty sure* it was the east wing." She met his eyes and stared at him. "I was wrong. It's the west wing. Go now and go fast. Hirst's life depends on it."

Aaron jumped behind Sarah and turned her around. He walked briskly down the hallway, dodging slow-moving patients and gurneys.

"I don't think you're going fast enough," Sarah said. "We have less than a minute to get set up by the door in the stairwell that leads outside."

Parkman ran ahead to clear a path.

Aaron pushed faster.

Chapter 43

Hirst got in his car and left the driver's side door open. The Los Angeles heat had pasted his shirt to his back. Inside the car, the heat was worse, soaking his shirt through with sweat.

He sat in the front seat while he asked for backup at the hospital. He lied, saying there had been sightings of Father Adams in and around the building.

"You better be right about this, Sarah," he whispered to himself.

Two units were dispatched.

Now he needed to locate two doctors and have them come to the door on the east side of the hospital. As far as Hirst knew, there would be several doors over there.

He slammed his car door shut and, after hitching up his pants, started across the parking lot, eager to get back inside the air-conditioned building.

A BMW cruised through the rows of cars, looking for a

spot. Waiting for Father Adams to show himself, Hirst slowed to let the car go by and watched as it parked in the row in front of him. He started walking again, going in between the BMW and a four-door Buick.

The BMW's door opened. Hirst looked back as the female driver pushed her hair behind her ears and then reached in to collect something else on the passenger seat. No one else was in the car. He turned back around, about to cross a grassy median, when the woman screamed.

Hirst spun back.

Father Adams, sans hat, stood behind him. His open black jacket exposed a series of tubes strapped to his abdomen. He aimed a gun at Hirst from two feet away. Hirst had been so focused on the BMW driver that he hadn't detected Adams creeping up behind him.

"Don't make any sudden moves," Adams said. "You're not the one I'm interested in."

"Then I'll be on my way. I've come to see my grandmother at the hospital. She's broken a hip."

"Bullshit." Sweat dripped into Adams's eyes. He blinked it away.

The driver of the BMW had gotten back in the driver's seat. She turned the car on, dropped it in reverse, and backed away. Father Adams didn't budge.

"You're here to see Sarah Roberts." Adams smiled. "I have no idea how she got everyone out of that church. I'll have to ask when I see her."

Hirst thought of his gun and cursed Sarah. Why had she been so adamant about disarming him? What could she have been thinking?

"Aren't you done yet? When will it be over?"

"I'm done when the woman who killed my brother is done."

"So what's the plan?" Hirst asked. "You gonna blow yourself up?"

"Where's Sarah?"

"Probably halfway home by now."

"You're lying. I called. I know she's in there." He gestured with his head toward the hospital. Then he lowered the gun to his waist, keeping the barrel pointed at Hirst. "Remove your weapon."

Maybe that's why Sarah took it.

Hirst showed his empty holster. "Don't have one on me."

"Bullshit. Guys like you always carry a gun. You must have an ankle holster."

Hirst raised his foot slowly and displayed his naked ankle, no holster. Then he repeated it for the other foot.

"I don't carry when visiting my grandmother at the hospital. Upsets her."

"You want to continue with that story, do you?"

"You don't expect to just walk into this hospital with all their security, take the elevator to Sarah's room and blow everything up, do you?"

"No. But you can."

"Yeah? How's that?"

"Turn around. Start walking. You'll lead the way. As we get close to the doors and people are milling around, I will hide my gun. Anything you do other than walk me directly to Sarah's room gets you killed. Once I'm with Sarah, I will empty my magazine and give you my gun. I will give you two minutes to clear the area of doctors and nurses before I set this off."

"What makes you think I will help you kill Sarah?"

"Because you, like every man, have a strong sense of self-preservation. You won't risk me pushing this button while I'm beside you. I'm dead already. Let me go and take that nuisance with me. I'll be out of your hair. Sarah, someone you barely know, will be gone, too. It'll all be officially over, and you can return to your life."

Sarah wanted two doctors to come to the side door in the east wing. She said Father Adams would show up, and Sarah had his weapon. Everything had been right so far. He had everything to lose by trying to be the hero and everything to gain by doing what Sarah had asked.

"Okay, fine," Hirst said. "We'll play it your way. But we don't walk in the main doors or even the emergency doors. There are too many people in both areas, and there'll be security. If one guard recognizes your face, it'll all end fast, and I don't want to go out like that."

Adams smiled, showing white teeth. "Fabulous idea. Turn around and start walking."

Hirst did as he was told. Once they passed the grassy median, they started across a wide concrete area where ambulances came and headed toward the east access with Hirst in the lead.

Sarah would be there waiting for them. But what then? Get his gun back? Hirst couldn't shoot Adams for fear of setting off the bomb strapped to his chest. Hirst's focus had to be the bomb. Whether they lived through this or not, keeping that bomb from going off inside the hospital had to be the priority.

Something nagged at him as he angled toward the east side of the massive building, with a plan to keep to the less populated areas. Something Sarah had said.

What the hell was it?

"Hey," Adams said.

Hirst slowed, then stopped. "What is it?"

"Go the other way."

"What way?" Hirst half turned to look at him. "The doors are right up there. Then I'll take you to Sarah's room."

Adams shook his head. "No. We do it my way."

"I thought we *were* doing it your way."

"Sarah can see things. She's some kind of precog. You're too determined for me. You didn't want the front doors. You immediately wanted the east side of the building. Even if Sarah's not involved in some way, I don't like it."

"What are you talking about? You think Sarah and I talked about you coming here? If that was the case, why didn't she tell a SWAT team to be waiting for you? Or a sniper in a tree? No, I'm taking you into the hospital because you've kidnapped me. I'm doing what you asked because I have no other choice."

"Me doth think he protests too much." Adams winked at him. "Start walking to the doors on the west side. It's either that or I'll kill you here and go to the front desk. Maybe they will listen to my little gun."

Hirst couldn't believe what he was hearing. He couldn't take Adams to the west side when Sarah would be waiting with his gun at the door fifty yards away.

Father Adams clicked the safety to the off position on his weapon.

"That was the sound of time," he said. "You're almost out of it."

Hirst had no choice. He couldn't let it end like this. He

couldn't die so pointlessly. All because he didn't want to walk to another door. There had to be more to life, to the universe, than dying because of a door choice.

He put one foot in front of the other and led Father Adams toward the west side doors, the whole time trying to figure out what else Sarah had told him. It was something to think about or something to remember.

What the hell was it?

Chapter 44

THERE WAS A SLIGHT jog at the end of the corridor, and then the double doors on the hospital's west side opened to a sunny afternoon.

"Now what?" Parkman asked.

"Tip me over."

"What?" Aaron nearly shouted.

"No questions! I need you to do it now. We've got thirty seconds or less."

Aaron and Parkman eased her wheelchair over until she rested sideways on the floor.

"Push me closer to the doors."

They complied.

"Now wheel my IV stand over here."

Aaron brought it over.

"Lay it down with the bag at my end, the gun near the wall."

"But you won't be able to reach it there."

"It isn't for me. No more delays. We're almost out of time." She pointed down the hall. "That stretcher two doors up. Bring it over here."

Parkman did as he was told, running back so fast with the stretcher that he almost ran into Sarah on the floor. She pulled the sheets down, intending to cover her face.

"Now. Both of you need to disappear. I'll be dead if either of you is seen. Get around that corner and keep people away from here for a couple of minutes. When a gun goes off, come running. Bring doctors, too."

"You can't be serious," Aaron said. "I can't leave you like this."

"Go now, or you'll get me killed."

Parkman grabbed Aaron's arm and twisted him around. "Dammit, Aaron. Love her another day. Listen to her now. Let's go."

Normally Aaron could've broken the hand that grabbed him before he got fully turned around. She was proud that he trusted Parkman enough not to lash out. She also adored how much he loved her, but he needed to listen to her in times like this.

It always seemed to come back to the same old question of acceptance. Aaron said he accepts her, but his actions tell another story. His internal struggle saddened her. Love and protect her by not letting her enter the cage to fight the tiger on her own was programmed into a man like Aaron. It was like trying to teach a rugged bear hunter who lived off the land to enter culinary school to be a chef in a fancy New York restaurant. Not impossible, but not likely to happen.

She covered her face with the sheets and waited. To an

outsider, it looked like a patient had tipped their wheelchair over, knocked their IV stand to the floor, and grabbed for a nearby gurney in an attempt to arrest their fall, only getting bed sheets for their effort.

Footsteps approached the doors from the outside.

She waited.

The door opened.

Someone stepped inside. Two someones.

It was time.

Another door opened nearby.

A man gasped on her right.

Another man on her left said, "Hold up."

Father Adams.

"But a patient has fallen."

Then the sheets were ripped away, and Sarah's face was exposed.

Chapter 45

As the doors on the west side got closer, Hirst snuck a look back. Father Adams still had the gun out but hidden at his waist.

Five feet from the hospital's west side entrance, Hirst couldn't figure out what he was forgetting. Sarah had told him to remember something specific. And with her waiting at the east wing with his gun, he was on his own. And what would happen when he took Adams up to her empty room?

He smiled as it came together for him. That had to be it. Sarah was on the east side of the building so she could escape unharmed. She was doing exactly what Hirst had asked her to do: leave. He would take Father Adams up to an empty room, and it would all be over.

He couldn't fault her for her decision. He had been pushing her to leave, and now she was cleared for takeoff. He'd have no way of defending himself in Sarah's empty hospital room.

Hirst put his hand on the door. Slowly, so as not to startle his kidnapper, he pulled it open, walked through, and held it for Adams. The door squeaked as it closed behind them.

A patient had fallen off a wheelchair in the corridor.

A door on the left opened, and a man in a white lab coat emerged. He gasped and turned toward the fallen patient.

Adams stepped close to Hirst, the tip of the gun touching the small of his back.

"Hold up," Adams said to the doctor.

"But a patient has fallen," the doctor responded. He lifted the sheet to expose Sarah's face.

Then it dawned on Hirst. Sarah had told him to remember Janice, his wife. When the moment was right, it would come to him. The bombs strapped to Adams. They were fakes, just like the one strapped to Janice's neck. Father Adams wasn't going to kill himself. He just wanted Sarah.

"You!" Father Adams yelled.

Sarah grabbed the IV stand and swung it toward the two men as Adams pulled the weapon away from Hirst's back. He brought it over Hirst's shoulder and aimed at Sarah.

The IV stand wasn't coming fast enough.

The doctor in the white lab coat stepped back, his hands raised, mumbling something.

"I finally get to end this," Adams shouted.

Self-preservation kept Hirst paralyzed. What if Sarah was wrong about the bombs? But what if she was right?

I swore never to doubt her again.

Hirst shrugged as the gun fired, enough of a bump to knock off the aim. The bullet chunked the tile floor behind Sarah's head.

The IV stand stopped at Hirst's feet, the grip of his weapon in view.

A crushing blow to the back of his head sent him crashing to the ground, where he sprawled across Sarah's legs.

"You were working together, I see," Father Adams said.

"Now take it easy," Aaron said from behind Sarah.

"What are you doing here?" Sarah asked.

"You told us to come after the first gunshot. You said bring doctors."

"Shit. I did say that, didn't I? Sorry. But now you have to leave again."

"Ah, can't do that."

Father Adams raised his arms to expose the bombs strapped to his chest. "Stay right where you are."

The doctor who had lifted Sarah's sheet turned and ran.

Hirst squirmed off Sarah's legs, edging toward the end of the IV stand to get to his gun. Sarah was defenseless, and everyone thought the bombs were real.

"Let's make a deal," Aaron said.

"No deal."

Hirst rolled, the back of his neck aching where Adams had hit him.

"The only deal any of you make is with God," Adams said. He turned back to Sarah. "But no matter what happens, you die first."

"Then do it, asshole," Sarah said, her face pensive, as if death was an engaging thought, even welcoming. "What are you waiting for?"

Father Adams's eyes bulged, and a vein on his forehead stuck out. He brought his weapon to bear on Sarah.

"Shoot her, and I'll kill you," Aaron said, his voice cold.

"So brave," Adams said. "Yet so stupid."

Hirst had the IV stand in his grasp, but the end of it was still too far to reach without drawing attention his way.

Adams's gun moved slightly, his aim now transferred to Aaron.

"No!" Sarah shouted.

Hirst reared up and swung the IV stand. It connected with Father Adams's ankle with a crack. Adams bent at the waist and screeched. He raised his gun once more, this time not hesitating to fire.

Hirst spun and rolled with the impact of the bullet in his shoulder. At first, there was no pain. Only the feeling that he had been punched with a sledgehammer. But he rolled with it, then rolled again, stopping at the base of the IV stand.

Adams's gun fired once more, loud in the narrow corridor. Hirst had no idea where that bullet went. He had to focus on his gun, taped to the bottom of the IV stand.

He twisted into position, pushed the IV stand to the left to achieve the needed angle, and grabbed the handle. His fingers wouldn't wrap around the butt of the weapon. His fingers weren't responding. He scanned his arm to examine the blood pouring out of his wound. The bullet must have damaged something that prevented him from using his hand. He was right-handed. He could not fire his weapon with his left, even if he wanted to.

The bottom of the IV stand was a silver disk that housed the wheels. In the way the IV stand lay on the floor, it would be virtually impossible for his left hand to get to the gun unless he flipped it all the way around.

Pain in his shoulder rolled in like a poisonous wave of

red.

Suddenly someone was on him. Someone had dove into him, landing on his shoulder. The world wavered in and out, his vision fading. He snapped back at the sound of a gun firing.

Aaron.

He had jumped on Hirst. His hand was wrapped around the taped-up gun at the base of the IV stand. Hirst's gun fired, and the bullet hit Father Adams in the center of the bombs strapped to his body.

Adams faltered back a step, looking down at the bloody mess seeping out of his chest.

Hospital security raced around the corner, weapons drawn.

"Put it down!" the first one yelled. "Put it down," he shouted again.

Father Adams looked up at them, his face calmer. "I'm going to blow the place up," he said.

When he reached for the bombs on his chest, Hirst shouted for the security guards to stand down. He shouted that the bombs were fakes.

But no one heard him over the sound of weapons fire.

Father Adams's body jerked like a marionette puppet governed by an insane puppeteer, the gun falling harmlessly from his grasp. Father Adams stayed on his feet for a few more seconds when the gunfire ceased.

Then he fell in a heap of blood and torn flesh.

Hirst lowered his head, shut his eyes, and let the world swim away. It was warmer down there and more comfortable.

Asleep, the pain stopped too.

Chapter 46

When Detective David Hirst woke up in his own hospital bed, more than a dozen people surrounded him.

"What's this?" he asked softly, his eyes half-lidded.

"Welcome to the land of the living," Parkman said.

"Yeah, great …"

Sarah stepped into view, a crutch under her arm. "You saved my life with your shoulder. I need to say thanks."

He tried to shrug, to show her his shoulder action, but it failed miserably.

"What happened to my shoulder?" Hirst asked, still dazed.

A doctor said, "You took a bullet, but we got it out. You'll be just fine. Even back on the job within a couple of months."

Hirst scanned the faces in the room. More than half of them were his colleagues from work.

"What are you guys all doing here?"

"We're here to congratulate you on nailing the priest killer," his old partner Paul said. "Who would've thought to strap a gun to the bottom of that IV stand believing that Adams would come for Sarah? Man, that was genius. Then to knock her over and out of the way. You saved her life and Aaron's and Parkman's. What I still can't figure out is how you shot him left-handed. You always sucked with your left hand."

Hirst looked at Aaron, who stood behind Sarah. Aaron offered him a subtle shake of his head. He turned to Parkman. His head moved in an almost imperceptible nod.

"Luck, I guess," Hirst said.

"Well, the media has picked up the whole story. You're a fucking hero, Hirsty."

"Don't call me that." Hirst winced at a sudden sharp pain in his side.

"It's been too long. We'll always call you Hirsty after all the beer you knocked back in your twenties."

"What else have the papers been saying?"

"How brilliant you were to call Parkman and Sarah in on this." Paul glanced at them and smiled. "Sarah's got quite the reputation, and even though there were mixed feelings about her, she got the front page for saving everyone in that church. She even allowed herself to be used as bait in the hospital to get the priest killer, even though she almost died a few times. Congratulations to all of you."

Everyone in the room clapped, the doctor included.

"We need to leave now," Sarah said.

"Where are you going?" Hirst asked.

"Home for a rest." She took Hirst's hand, leaned down,

and whispered, "Thanks for listening to me. Because of you, we all made it." She met his eyes.

"The thanks goes to you," Hirst said. "For my wife, and getting me out of that church and—"

"Shhh," she said, shaking her head. "You asked for our help. We came. We helped. But now we have to leave."

"Be well. Stay in touch."

Sarah stepped away. Aaron followed her.

Parkman put a hand on Hirst's good shoulder and moved a red toothpick to the other side of his mouth. "Take care of yourself."

"What is it with you and your toothpicks?" Hirst asked.

"Call us if you ever need anything again," Parkman said, ignoring Hirst's question.

"You do the same. If I can ever return the favor …"

At the door, Sarah and Aaron waited. They were gone minutes later, and Hirst was alone with his colleagues and his reality.

The case was closed. It was truly over. And he had been shot for the first time in his life. It wasn't so bad. A little time off work. A long rest. Maybe a little vacation.

Maybe he would head up along the coast to Santa Rosa when he left the hospital.

There were a few people who live and work in Santa Rosa that he needed to buy dinner for.

Maybe a few dinners.

He could take Janice. They could make a holiday out of it.

The good Lord knew he needed a vacation.

Chapter 47

When they got to the car, Aaron helped Sarah in and stored her crutch in the back with him.

"Where to?" Parkman asked.

"Home."

"Home as in Santa Rosa?"

Sarah nodded. "I need to heal. I need a break. I can't keep this up on a crutch. When I'm trained better, running and active, I have a job to do."

"What job?" Aaron asked.

"I want to locate that cop I once knew from my childhood. I have a score to settle."

"That doesn't sound good. You can't run around settling scores with cops."

"Cop or not, he has to be made accountable for what he did."

Parkman started the car and drove out of the hospital

parking lot.

"I wanted to ask you, Sarah," Aaron said from the backseat. "How did you know how it would go down in the hospital? How did you know to tape the gun and to be at the west side?"

"Vivian."

"I gathered that much. But I hadn't seen any notes. How did she communicate all that to you?"

Sarah watched the landscape pass by through her window.

"She's mostly in my head now."

That was greeted by silence. Parkman stole a glance her way.

"We can still use automatic writing," Sarah said. "But Vivian has learned to insert thoughts into my consciousness. It almost feels like a twin is speaking to me through telepathy. I know the thought is in my mind, but it isn't original."

"Wow," Aaron said.

"The only problem is that I also get her memories from when she was here on Earth with our parents."

"How is that a problem? You now have two sets of childhood memories with Caleb and Amelia."

"Vivian was brutally raped and murdered."

Another moment of silence.

Then Parkman said, "I'm so sorry."

"I can almost see the man's face when it happened." Sarah watched a Ford Mustang pass them on the left, paying only enough attention to see it go by. "Sometimes I have a Vivian nightmare." She focused on the Mustang again. "While I'm awake."

"Oh man," Aaron whispered.

"To quell those thoughts or help ease them, I need to find that cop. He has to pay for what he did."

"What about Vivian's murderer?"

"He died in Europe. I can't re-kill him as much as I would like to."

"Parkman is a solid investigator," Aaron said. "He'll help you with whatever you need, as will I."

"I hate being haunted by these horrid thoughts that aren't mine, but I'm happy with how close I've gotten to my sister. We can talk without anyone listening now. Messages are faster and easier. But it hurts my heart so much to feel what Vivian went through in her last lonely moments as a flesh and blood body. I'll kill every rapist I can for what happened to her."

"Okay, Sarah, but first healing."

She nodded. "First healing. I can't chase the asshole like this."

An image floated through her mind. She closed her eyes and held her temples.

"What is it?" Parkman asked.

The image intensified. A fist coming down. Blood. The man's face. She recognized him. More blood. Vivian's clothes ripped off. Her young body was exposed. Her cry for her mother. Then ...

Sarah forced her eyes open and clenched her fists. "I can't handle it sometimes. It's too much. Vivian tries to insulate me, but she can't to keep our connection strong."

"What did you see?"

"Death. Murder. Her rape."

"I'm sorry, Sarah."

"Me too, Parkman. Me too. Now that I'm redeemed, I feel like I'm *The Haunted*."

"Sounds like it."

The car raced toward Santa Rosa and a dismal future.

Afterword

DEAR READER,

I think it needs to be said that I have no personal issue, grudge against, or angst toward Catholicism as a religion or any other religion. Because Catholicism is one of the largest religions in the world, with more than 1.6 billion members, and it's one of the bloodiest religions, I chose it to be the focus of this novel.

When I read in early 2014 that the United Nations had requested archived evidence on the abuse of tens of thousands of children by Catholic priests, I was astounded that the Vatican denied this request. Actually, I'm shocked that denial is even allowed. The United Nations accused the Vatican of turning a blind eye to decades of sexual abuse of children by priests and ridiculed church officials' "code of silence" imposed on clerics as the church moved abusers from church to church in an attempt to handle the abuse internally.

Child molestation is an absolute disgrace. The fact that it happens at all makes me ashamed to be human. How can an adult hurt a child in such a way, all for a moment's selfish pleasure? It's an absolute abomination. Once this horrific act has occurred, and investigators have enough evidence or a statement to name a suspect, that person needs to be held accountable for what they have done in the most brutal fashion afforded by law.

The fact that these suspects represent a church, whichever church that might be, is more than astounding. It's atrocious.

But what's worse is that the church protects these individuals by "Handling it internally."

So I decided to, fictitiously, in the novel you just read, kill off a few of these assholes.

As a writer, I often find my tales are based on something I've read in the news that has incensed me. Whether the content is positive or negative, scary or happy, my novels are all based on research, personal experience, beliefs, ideas, ideals, and, ultimately, imagination.

For me, every story begins with a *What if ...*

I've been on a spiritual journey since I was very young. It started with Sunday school at the tender age of six or seven. Long yellow buses picked me up on Sunday mornings and drove me to a large building with huge windows—not a church—where they would scare the shit out of me. A yardstick, an agenda of fear, and a side serving of guilt for being born were my first experiences with religion.

By the age of nine, I was told that I had to ask Jesus into

my heart or I would die and burn in a lake of fire, and I would never see my parents ever again. It was explained to me that because of what Adam and Eve did in the Garden of Eden, women were punished with the pain of childbirth, and men were punished with the pain—supposedly in their backs —of providing and working to feed and clothe their families. Because of what happened in that fabled Garden all those years ago, we're all sinners. Even as we're born, we are born into sin, no matter how nice, or hard we try to lead a good, solid life.

I left that church—cult—in 1979. It wasn't until six years later, at the age of sixteen, that I wanted to understand God, myself, and religion more. So I began Bible study. I spent time at a Pentecostal church where they spoke in tongues. I examined the history of the Quakers who shook on the church floor. In my late teens, I learned about Mormons by spending a week in a Mormon family's home and visiting their church, where we drank the blood of Christ and ate his body. I learned how a man named Joseph Smith saw an angel in the early 1800s and began the Mormon religion.

Religion began to seem a little crazy to me.

Ultimately this all led to my early twenties, where I examined Buddhism, Judaism, and Islam. Karen Armstrong is a wonderful author on Religion who wrote, *The Battle for God: A History of Fundamentalism*, among others. I also found Deepak Chopra's *How to Know God* a moving experience.

After visiting various churches and reading a myriad of books on the subject, I found David Gersten's *Are You Getting Enlightened, or Losing Your Mind?* This book debunked what many modern religions stood for and explained how many were based on pagan religions and how even things like Easter were a pagan festival. The symbolic story of the son's death on the cross and his rebirth was told countless times in the ancient world.

A Sumerian goddess, Ishtar, was hung naked on a stake and was resurrected and ascended, as reportedly Jesus did, too. One of the oldest resurrection myths was about Horus, an Egyptian who was born on December 25.

As this is slowly becoming a debate on religion, which I did not intend to have here, I will conclude that there was no mention of Easter in the New Testament. Easter's date is not fixed. It is dictated by the phases of the moon, which is quite pagan.

Having said all that, I'm not advocating for people to walk away from their current religion or belief system. We're all at a different level spiritually, and I have seen the church help many people in their time of need. Mother Teresa is a perfect example of what modern religion is capable of.

Belief and faith are very personal things. As much as I won't push my beliefs on someone, I don't want their beliefs pushed on me. As the novel says, beliefs are simply opinions you're unwilling to reconsider.

In my opinion, there is a higher power. Most of what I believe is what you heard Sarah tell Parkman in the hospital scene. We're all here living our own blueprint, and everyone in your life is there because you wrote it that way.

As Sarah said in the novel, religion is for people who don't want to go to Hell, and spirituality is for people who have been there.

I believe in the other side, which is what led me to create Sarah and Vivian in the first place. Vivian was inspired by my brother, who died when I was fourteen years old. I mention him in my novel that he inspired, *A Murder in Time.*

My brother has come to me several times in dreams. When I was eighteen, I woke up one morning with a vivid dream of him stuck in my head. He had come bearing a warning that I needed to pack a spare pair of pants for work that day. I wouldn't normally need an extra pair of pants at my job, but I decided to humor the memory of my brother, now gone from this world only four years at the time.

I rode my 18-speed mountain bike to work every day. On that particular day, as I negotiated the final turn into my workplace, the front tire caught on pebbles, slipped out from under me, and I smashed into the pavement going at least twenty miles an hour. While sliding along the hard ground, my thick wad of keys caught on something sticking up and slashed the length of my pants. Unhurt for the most part, I only had a tiny cut or two on my hands that had, by reflex, saved my face. I stood up to examine the damage to my bike. As I got to my feet, my pants slipped off me, completely shredded. There wasn't a single cut on my legs, though. Needless to say, I thanked my dead brother for saving my ass while slipping into my extra pair of pants.

So whatever you believe, whatever gets you through your day, I hope and pray that you're happy, motivated by goodness, and not guilt. That you're fulfilled or working toward fulfillment and that you're healthy.

Dear reader, you don't have to have faith. You don't have to believe in God because he believes in you. As individuals, you don't even have to believe in that.

All I ever ask is that you believe in Sarah and have fun with her as she moves on to *The Haunted*, where she comes face to face with the man who molested her all those years ago.

Then we're on to *The Unlucky*, where Vivian takes on an intrusive role in Sarah's life and makes her do things that will surprise the hell out of people.

Sarah is in for a world of pain, bad luck, anguish, torment, and ultimately love as she finds her way, book by book, further into Aaron's arms.

Keep reading because one day, Aaron and Sarah need to get married. And what will a pregnant Sarah be like? And the catastrophe that befalls her during her pregnancy is mind-blowing. I can tell you they eventually have a lovely daughter. You'll meet her in the books to come.

But I'm getting ahead of myself here. We shouldn't be talking about the fifteenth book and the nineteenth book. They're all coming in 2015, with another host of books in 2016, with my aim to take the Sarah Roberts Series as far as I can for many years to come.

Until the next book, I say farewell and ask only one thing of you.

Ask questions.

That is all.

Just ask questions.

The more you ask, the more will be revealed to you.

Religion, as with many things, does not hold up well to scrutiny. Research. Learn. Digest what you've learned. Make your own conclusions. And then live your life the way you want to live it and not by someone else's design.

Get caught reading …

Jonas Saul

P.S. Detective David Hirst was named after two of my high school friends. Dave Darling and Doug Hirst. I met them both in grade eight, and we're still friends. As in almost every novel, I like to honor friendship this way. Thanks, guys, for all the memories. The days of our youth are over, but the memories live on. Now, have a beer already.

About Jonas Saul

Jonas Saul is the bestselling author of the Sarah Roberts Series—more than two million sold!—and has written and published over sixty thrillers. After acquiring an agent, he signed several deals in Los Angeles, with MadRiver Pictures optioning his Sarah Roberts Series— over forty books!—(currently in development).

Jonas has often outranked Stephen King and Dean

Koontz on Amazon over the past decade. He's regularly invited to be a guest speaker, teacher, or workshop presenter at international writing conferences and film festivals worldwide. He hosts an annual writer's retreat in Greece, where he currently lives. He focuses his teaching on how to get tension and emotion in every scene, on every page, how he made it as a creator/writer, the path to success in this business, and the pitfalls to avoid. He also hosts a reading retreat in Greece with guest authors, yoga retreats, and hiking retreats. Visit the Imagine Greece Retreats website at www.imaginegreeceretreats.com, or email him directly to discuss an opportunity to join one of the retreats at jonas@imaginegreeceretreats.com.

Jonas is also a professional freelance editor. He works for several publishers and does private editing for clients, with many testimonials on his website at www.imaginepress.org, which details each author's response to Jonas's editing skills. Email Jonas directly for an editing quote at editor@imaginepress.org.

To book Jonas for a speaking engagement at a writer's conference/festival, to have him on your jury at a film festival, or even to say hello, email Jonas directly at jonassaul@icloud.com.

For updates on releases, hit the "Follow" button on Amazon or Bookbub, and join Jonas on Facebook, where he's most active.

Contact Jonas Saul

Linktree: Find me here

Email: jonassaul@icloud.com